Shadows That Tempt

GITTE TAMAR

BTW LLC

To those who have dealt with harsh mistreatment by someone who boastfully claims their neverending love, you will never regret placing your individuality above and retaining your cherished self-love.

Acknowledgments

Thank you to each of my family and friends, you already know who you are, so I will refrain from listing each of your specific names. Just know I will forever be thankful for each one of you who provided me with never-ending troves of love and emotional support.

Thank you to all of my readers for continuing to embark on this journey with me. I am forever indebted to you.

Contents

Chapter One

WE MEET AGAIN

1889, Philmont England

Morning light plunders every window in the boudoir and warms each eggplant-purple crushed-velvet curtain. Jarred from my slumber, my body is slow to wake, and my motor skills are dull. Silently I lie resting on top of the covers of my cold fortress. The trials of sickening grief pelt each shifting thought that rummages through my core—recollections of the grotesque images I viewed the night before. An aching sensation falls over my head and down each rib. I am alone. Frantically I clutch at my chest for the large locket around my neck, and finding it with my fingertips brings me comfort. While my mouth exhales a long yawn, my eyes cast a glance at my bare feet and take notice of my bodice. As I'm still wearing my full corset from the previous night, my waist resembles that of a malnourished child, and the excruciating pain from the overflexed bones is unbearable.

Ghastly, I think. *Whoever thought of this contraption must have been a man.*

In an attempt to distract me from the pain in my bruised ribs, I abruptly shift my focus to the tiny glimmers of light attempting to enter through the nearby windows. The idea that today may be the time of my grand surrender weighs heavily on my eyelids. Chiming bells ring from the church down the street, but their sound is muffled through the four walls.

Today is my wedding day.

Chime, ching, chime, the bells sing.

Each ring jumps up an octave higher than before and reminds me of a stepping stool with no purpose. If society deems that this song should bring forth joy and jubilance, why does my heart not comply? All the beats appear to be in tune, playing chipper melodies, so shouldn't I want the message to resonate with me? From a philosopher's standpoint, is that what I should sense, or does my melancholy state stem from the fact that I do not revel in my past? To be honest, I wish this marriage were my last, but I know deep down this shall not be the end of my arduous path.

Shouldn't I be happy? I ponder. *Isn't this what they groomed me to be?*

I can't help thinking back to my dream. Why was it so vivid? What did it mean? Like a mother's criticizing words, the sound of scurrying feet in the hall and a creaking door cut through my rambling thoughts. Like wars pause with a white flag held high, my mind ceases fire as I become the model of passivity, something long expected of me.

"Who is it?" I ask.

Let me take a moment to address the peculiarity of my timid response compared to my genuine, confident nature. I know it may be confusing since it is unbefitting my typical self-reliant character. Still, wherever I am, I intentionally adjust my perceived tone to something more subdued so I appear helpless to others. Rather than advertise myself as freethinking and intellectual, I must maintain my presence as a lady if I am to be received well and continue to marry.

"It is I, Joseline, the chambermaid. I'm here to help you prepare for your special day."

Oh, good God, I completely forgot about her, chuckling to myself as I glimpse down at my outfit. "Weren't you supposed to be of service last night? I dare say I woke up in some of the items I donned yesterday," I call through the door.

"Yes, true, miss, but you were rather stubborn last night and wouldn't allow me in the room. If I may say, you were quite persistent with dismissing me. You mentioned needing to talk to a friend, miss, but no one was here."

Her scrambling to cover her negligence makes my eyes roll in unison a dozen times, and her existence felt like a parody to me. Aren't we past the point of needing such help? I mean, I have two functional hands and feet. Even though I believe Joseline's job is pointless, I must acknowledge that no matter how unfulfilling her work may appear to me, it's probably the highlight of her existence. Although the notion is depressing, I must respectfully comply with the times. As I brush off my ill-thought ideas, I relax my breath and change my attitude from spiteful to thankful.

"Come in, child," I call through clenched teeth as I turn my throbbing head to face the door.

After the creaky bedroom door opens wide, revealing a small woman. Surprisingly, she looks just shy of seventeen years old. When I arrived late last night by horse-drawn carriage, in my inebriated state, I pictured her as an old hag. Quite honestly, I hadn't planned on becoming unduly intoxicated on my long journey to my new home, but there's something I must confess to everyone listening to my thoughts. We all know I have kept no secrets regarding the fact that this is not my first marriage, so I will continue to divulge on the subject. There is a valid reason I have engaged in numerous matrimonies; it should be evident that I favor being a recurring widow.

Trust me when I say each of their passings was more peaceful than the last. You may wonder how I know this for certain. Well, it is quite simple: I killed them. Naturally, when the time seems right later in the narrative, I will get to each of their reprehensible stories and clarify the why for my actions. In the meantime, let me explain the small matter of my intoxicated state during my carriage ride. If I met you on the street, I would tell you I've never removed the sizable locket from my neck because it is the last memory of my wonderful family before I was orphaned. I will let you in on a bit of a secret: the story is false. There are no cherished family photos within the ornate silver confinement. Husband number one gave me the necklace; if you open the locket, you'll see our initials engraved inside. Since I am committed to remaining honest with you, I also will disclose that the cursive letters are not the first thing you will see. Minute amounts of organic matter fill the encasement, cover the scrolling, and must be removed to reveal the engraving. That topic leads me in a full circle to the cause of my inebriated state last night.

Locked away inside the piece of rich jewelry are troves of uncleaned poppy seeds. If one harvests the pods before they're fully ripe, high amounts of opioids will soak the coating of each seed, and when ingested, they can be perfectly lethal. You may wonder how I made this brilliant discovery. Only having daughters made my mother resentful. As a direct result of her indignation, the sound of each daughter's cry provoked her to become increasingly ill-tempered. Desperately trying to tolerate her children, she regimentally gave them poppy seeds for sedation. As she upped the frequency of the dosages, her garden couldn't keep up. Impatient by the plants' slow production, she harvested a few unripe pods early. Her selfish nature made her complacent regarding the plant's strength and resulted in near deaths—including mine. After that, I educated myself on the intricacies of the seeds by reading multiple books on apothecaries. My knowledge became instrumental in my later marriages.

As you digest the new information bestowed upon your eyes, please do not view me as a monster. I assure you the seeds provide a tolerable way to perish, and unlike most, being altruistic, I practice what I preach. To ensure each new batch is adequately compounded, I always take it upon myself to ingest a nonlethal dosage to ensure the victim's initial high will be enjoyable. This explains my incoherent state while exiting the carriage and why I nodded off almost entirely clothed. When I took the typical trial dosage of seeds from the new harvest, the crop must have been more potent than usual. As my eyes roamed over the chambermaid, the thought that I would not have to use as many to finish her off made my lips quiver.

Joseline's body is clothed in a musty-gray standard uniform with all the layers decently fitting her tiny frame. The annoying voice projected from her lungs matches her average face. Her smallish brown eyes sit close together and bring to mind bodies of mud as they pool at the base of her other mountainous pinched features. Proudly storming into the room, she carries a gaudy oversize white wedding gown with bustling ruffles.

The realization I'm on husband number five sinks in, causing agony and terror to rise through the blood I chastise. Shouldn't I be happy instead of feeling humdrum? I mean, shouldn't I deem I have won?

Joseline sighs heavily as she races across the room to hang the gown in the wardrobe, her rushing energy causing her to stumble. If she could view deep inside my core, she would see what I have gone through and, in return, be thankful for her position in society. As soon as she hangs the heavy garment, her feet go on a lively spree around the room as she uncovers each window. As she pulls each velvet curtain open, bright light floods the chamber at the speed of frenzied sailors jumping from a sinking ship, and my headache worsens.

"Can you believe today is the day, miss?" she says.

The combination of harsh light and her shrill voice causes my wincing eyes to close. Trying to avoid nausea, I stare up at the tented boards of the canopy bed, and reaching next to me, I grab a pillow and place it over my head to subdue my heightened senses. Finished with this task, Joseline makes her way closer. As she approaches, the sound of each footstep striking the polished wooden floors grows unbearable. The pillow is snatched away without notice, and I'm left uncovered, lying face-to-face with her. The sight is unpleasant to my eyes.

"I can't fathom how excited you must be. I can only dream that one day I will get married," she states.

Oh, I'm excited, but not because of what you're referencing. The thought forms a condescending smile on my lips.

She isn't privy to the fact that this is my fifth betrothal; in all fairness, no one is. If acquaintances from my past and present were aware of one another, I would not have successfully attained solicitations from new prospects. Even if you have achieved status through marriage, being a widow is often stigmatized. I have had four prior marriages end in my husband's premature demise, which, if disclosed, would signal countless red flags to future courting prospects. I should tell you that all of my husbands have been quite wealthy. Still, their heinous personalities made their pockets seem unequivocally empty; society's pressure to marry made me a fiend for something I never truly desired. When I was a girl, people often told me my looks would hinder my future financial stability and I had to accept a fate of economic despair. Throughout my awkward adolescence, their cruel belittlement of my unique features proved to be quite ironic, as I exquisitely blossomed in every respect by age twenty. Reluctantly I will furnish you with a synopsis of the past to better explain my cynicism. I agree to provide you with some inside knowledge of my misery-filled childhood, referencing each family member by position, for they do not deserve to be identified by the human attribute of a name.

Counting me, five blood relations were residing within the estate. My father was always half rats; my mother thought she was a parish pickax; my middle sister was mediocre; the youngest atrocious; and then there was me, who was quite hopeless. Believe my words when I say my descriptions of them are polite assessments. Even in their deceased state, they are all insufferable, which is challenging to accomplish.

Not a single household member showed me the love a child requires, and that alone was enough to fuel my resentment.

My parents believed they must marry off their daughters for wealth to uphold the family surname. They didn't account for the notion that we lived in a small town, causing the name they cherished to mean nothing to anyone of importance in the world. Let me say this little factual bit ended up working to my advantage. Imagine being told all your existence that you are ugly and your sisters will marry above you. After ten plus years of hearing those words, you become discouraged. Embracing my unfortunate appearance, I versed myself in other activities deemed inappropriate for my sex, and reading became my favorite pastime.

Do not get in a fluster; I am one step ahead of you and already know what you think. *Gasp! A woman who reads is absurd.* My family had the same view toward the subject matter, and my parents were outraged to discover my love for books. Each week, my father burned a book from his library to prove a contentious point. Luckily for him, the heinous act didn't detour me from learning; rather, it inspired me. With every work of literature turned to ash, I taught myself to read faster. I wanted to absorb the entire library before the flames could eat them. Rather than aiding their intention to control me, my parents' actions provided them unwelcome outcomes. As I grew more enlightened regarding the possibilities beyond four confining walls, I wanted nothing more than to break free of their oppression. My many nights spent amassing knowledge ended up not being as lonely as I assumed it would.

Each night, when my father took his last sip of whiskey and lost consciousness on top of his desk, I'd quietly enter his study to read. One cold winter's eve, I carried on with my routine, unaware that my life would forever change. When I entered his study, the candles in the room's corner were extinguished without provocation, leaving me in darkness, and I became intrigued. Accompanying the dismissal of the warm flickering light was a mysterious voice that offered me comfort, and with its words, each of the candles' flames returned. As I was an impressionable child, that moment changed my life. Without a doubt, I was never the same from that night forward. The benevolent voice mentored me and expanded my knowledge with each book I read, allowing me the edification to take flight. For that reason, I was indebted to the voice I called my friend and desired that our encounters continue indefinitely.

I made a strict promise to meet with the shadowy figure each night, and with age, my life shifted in a direction I never dared imagine. As I delved into the pages of yet another novel depicting a creature similar to Dracula, I gazed over the top of the cover at a new suitor entering the parlor in the Bonnet estate. His presence permanently changed the trajectory of my path. Before I saw this man in the flesh, the voice in the shadows told me someone would arrive to help rid my life of misery, but I wasn't aware of the exact details until the story began to unfold. At first, the charming gentleman offered my youngest sister his hand in matrimony. Then, after an odd series of events, he shifted to my other sister as a replacement bride. Unlike my dimwitted family, I had read many descriptive works on the psychology of psychopathy.

The man who entered our lives, Daniel Manley, fit this bill perfectly.

When he first entered the parlor, I smelled his stench of death. His finicky twitches and clenching jaw made me realize he fought many demons trying to control him. His bouts of easily triggered anger combined with vast manipulation were only a couple of his flaws. Because of his well-kempt appearance, the rest of my family willingly saw past the warning signs that seemed evident to me. Then the news that my youngest sister had run away confirmed my suspicions. The thought that my youngest, greediest sibling would run away from a man of such wealth was absurd. Before I go much further, let me interject and say I do not lament what happened to my sister; she deserved every bit of what was done to her, and the world is a better place without her.

When Daniel came to claim the next of us in line for his replacement bride, I realized I had little time left to make my departure. Rather than subject myself to being a sitting duck waiting for the slow jaws of an alligator to attack, I ran and didn't look back.

When I slipped through my bedroom window to make my escape, the only possession I took with me was a sizable hardbound atlas. Leaving with only the clothes on my back and an atlas may seem quite foolish, but there was more to the book than meets the eye. Hidden between the pages was a cache of money that I plundered from my father's secret desk drawer of gambling hordes. Each night when I crept into the study to read, I would gently push my drunkenly dozing father to the side just enough to access the hiding spot, taking only enough as not to be noticed. I had amassed a small fortune by the time of my departure due to my father's alcohol-induced memory and secrets surrounding his vile habits. Without my friend's direction, I would have never known about the secret compartment, let alone its contents, and for that, I am forever grateful. In that instance of time, my parents' lack of care for me ended up working well in my favor. Since they rarely solicited me for marriage, I found it easy to stay under the radar when asking others for help to arrange my transportation to flee. Using the map as a reference point and a hired carriage, I was able to find my way in the direction of some distant cousins living in a small village called Hillstead in Northern England. By the time of my arrival, the news had traveled of my family's great massacre, and my cousin's consoling nature played well in my favor. I couldn't help smirk at the thought that I was, for once, the fortunate one, and their pity served me well.

I turned eighteen within a month of being taken in as their ward. Due to the loss of my entire family, a two-year mourning period seemed appropriate, and I can honestly state that I cherished every moment of the solitude. Upon its unwelcome completion, I was considered ready to be thrust into society as an agreeable prospect for suitors. The social buzz surrounding my worth grew with every solicitation, and I salute my family's stupidity for adding to my value. Nearly every available man in the upper echelon wanted to wed the last survivor of the Bonnet massacre, and I became the ultimate prize to have upstate. My husbands' gruesome deaths were not in vain. They allowed me to have the life the shadow figure had declared I deserved, and by their removal, I granted other women an opportunity to avoid a life they did not deserve. Though I relish the lavish life I've attained through my friend's assistance, as well as beneficial tragedy, I cannot forget the scream that resonates in my mind. To this day, I have a recurring dream portraying what would have happened if I hadn't run away that night several years ago.

Every night the repetitious thought plagues my mind, and my walking feet are always the driving instigator of the final narrative. Meandering through the darkness, I reach the road's midpoint leading to town. I pause, and an achy stabbing sensation batters my intestines, each jolting sense of guilt stemming from deep within my gut. I attribute the plummeting feeling echoing in my stomach to the fact that my family is in grave danger. Instead of following through with my escape, Mr. Daniel Manley's enchanting voice possesses my feet, the melodic timbre luring me to the front door of his estate like a siren call. My fixating eyes analyze each knot trapped within the dark wooden entry. The door abruptly opens, and Daniel's face greets me. His sadistic smirk reminds me of my shadowed friend, and its familiarity wraps a comforting blanket around my soul.

As he ushers me into the foyer, my nose is immediately met with the unforgettable stench of decaying flesh. Although most people would be terrified, I feel welcomed by the sensational fear and wafting stench. Across the room, I see my familiar friend perched in the corner. Before I finish this story, I must disclose that the next bit of my recollection is slightly blurred. Even warbled, however, the symbolism is immensely influential in my current way of living. Sitting around the elegant dining room table, set for an ornate feast, I am joined by all the deceased. Each of the gruesome ways my family has perished is displayed upon their nearly unrecognizable faces. Daniel stands dead center on top of the table, performing around an elaborate chandelier. My shadow friend heckles him from the corner during the grand finale, provoking him to join the others in death.

Daniel fulfilled his purpose in the shadowy entity's narrative, and for me to go forth with mine, he needs to be discarded, and the chapter involving his story closed. When I observe his body hanging before me in each reprise, I do not shed a tear. Instead, the swaying sensation presents in my mind as a visually pleasing pendulum that relaxes my thoughts. As I watch him take his last breath, the constraints around my limbs loosen, freeing my body from my seat. Detecting a dry sensation in my throat, I grab a bottle of wine from the table. As I take my first sip, I hear someone whisper my name from the hallway. Wandering in the voice's direction, I find a bare room that houses a wired mannequin wearing an imported white gown. Drawn by the beauty of the silk fabric, I move closer.

Scanning down, I realize the expensive attire has replaced my muted clothing, and the sight brings me peace. After setting the bottle of wine on the floor, I take a single spin in the elegant gown, and the fluttering skirt topples over the glass container, spilling its crimson contents across the floorboards. As my eyes follow the scarlet river, I can't help but imagine it to be bodily fluid from a slaughtered corpse; the thought brings a rushing warmth to my bones, and I realize that the missing piece holding me back from happiness is bloodshed. I feel complete.

The detailed account appeared in my dreams the first night I slept at my cousins' estate, and the image behind my eyelids felt vividly real. As I continually forced myself to analyze the nightly depiction, I realized the message sent by my shadowy friend told me how I was to do his bidding.

"Are you well, miss?" Joseline asks.

The sound of her timid voice stops my ranting mind from forging on with its philosophical spiral, and my vision is cleared. As each eye regains focus, I'm met with Joseline's swinging hands fanning my face with the surrounding air. Her assumption that I am unwell miffs me, and I draw in a heap of air to clear my throat.

"Yes, I am quite well," I reply.

"Very good."

My right eye flinches as her hands move away from my face. What is wrong with me? Is it possible I am not like the rest? You heard her statement as well as I; she wishes she were me, with the looming wedding and beautiful gown. Hell, maybe I would feel the same if I'd been dealt her cards. Noticing she's still staring at me; I force my lips to form a painful smile. Having been through this process so often, I've disregarded the emotions one should exhibit on such an important day, sitting here in my gloating misery when I should be stricken with joy. Soon I will marry another disagreeable man and wear yet another white scalloped gown structured with dainty white lace. To not give away the dark secrets in my mind, I must provide this child with the emotionally charged show she desires.

Looking toward the hanging white gown, I release the theatrics. "I couldn't be happier with the design. Indeed, it embodies every dream I ever dreamt of as a small child while planning my future matrimony." Each word leaves my lips like a blossoming rose.

Taking a beat of pause, I wait for Joseline's reaction to my excellent performance. Like clockwork, her eyes slowly turn to admire the gown, and she fights back happy tears. Since I can be honest with you and no one else, I must disclose that the gown is not one of my favorites; in fact, it is quite the contrary. Even though the ensemble initially presents as expensive, I know it is not rich by the fine details. With its gaudy construction, the flowing layers of the material are a tacky showpiece rather than a reflection of monetary value.

"It is exquisite, isn't it?" she says, gawping in awe at the gown.

Pretending to comfort her, I hoist myself off the bed, move closer to her slight frame, and lightly touch my hand against her back. "It shall be yours, child, after the wedding."

Joseline falls silent as she allows each of my words to seep into her ears. Swiftly she pivots to look at me, and I notice she is at a loss for words, which touches my soul.

"I insist," I state, taking her by the shoulders and positioning her to face the dress.

"I don't know what to say," she replies.

"Nothing. You don't need to speak a word to anyone. This shall be our merry little secret."

Immediately I know I have her right where I want her to be, and she will be indebted to me. Joseline could be labeled an accomplice with the dress in her custody and stand-in for me as a scapegoat if the need arises. The thought of getting my way is the only thing that puts a genuine smile on my lips, and together we share certain happiness.

"Shall I get dressed?" I ask.

Before I can say another word, Joseline plucks the marital costume from the hanger, and we're off to the races. Her hands slip the bulky material over my head and swiftly cinch me into my suffocating fate. Her eyes display a sense of pride at her accomplishing the task of getting me ready. I look up to see her pointing to the self-standing mirror in the corner.

Oh, yes, this is where I'm supposed to ogle myself with overwhelming excitement.

Trying to quench her thirsty anticipation, I entertain her. Slowly I move toward the mirror, then wait until my back faces her before releasing a smirk. The feeling of dictating her happiness intrigues me, and I wish to bask in the euphoric high if possible. Feeling the tips of my toes reach the mirror's edge prompts my lungs to take a deep exhalation. To disguise my disgust for the garment, I need to mentally prepare myself for what I'm about to see. Once I finish collecting my thoughts, I leisurely lift my head to glance at my reflection.

Joseline moves behind me and glances around me in the mirror. "You truly are a vision. Sir Fitz is the luckiest gentleman in the world to have a bride as beautiful as you."

The compliments act as fuel for my eccentric ego. In my attempt to fish for more, I strike various poses in the mirror. After taking a few spins, I watch the momentum swish the bustling skirt like it did in my dream. At this moment, I know nothing can ruin my happiness.

"May I ask you something, miss?" says Joseline.

Trapped by my gorgeous reflection staring back at me, I watch my jawline as I slowly nod.

"Who was the friend you said you must speak with last night?"

As the question echoes in my skull, my eyes fixate on the shadowed corner of the room. As I may still need Joseline's assistance with my eventual escape, it takes everything in me not to kill her.

"The long trip must have gotten to me," I tell her. "It was no one, my sweet child."

Chapter Two

ISNT THAT JUST MARVELOUS

As Joseline continues to make awkward eye contact with me, contentment overcomes the curiosity in her eyes. Waiting for her gaze to break is torturous, like a never-ending chore. Each time I sense her eyes dropping from strain and fatigue, she surprises me by glaring another minute longer. Many would consider my opinion entirely credible. For that reason, I will cave to your wishful thinking and state my perception. To quench the entirety of your thirst, I will willingly further explain my thoughts on the matter of Joseline's behavior.

The child has a cloud of naivete surrounding her head like a thunderstorm, causing her doe eyes to radiate a glassy sheen. In all fairness, that's not my point of contention with the girl. It is merely a general observation a great many others might also make if asked about her face's insipid appearance. As my point revolves solely around her peculiar etiquette, that is the last observation I will make regarding her aesthetics. From now on, every ounce of my assessment will strictly relate to Joseline's actions or mannerisms. I will start by explaining why I find the entire blandly dressed package repulsive. In judging her, I have compared her movements to those of others I have encountered, and my comparative thoroughness should comfort you.

Unlike most of the world, I do not cast judgment without a valid reason. Before finalizing my opinions, I use academia to build each case. For those who still do not understand my justification process, you are lucky you know me now in my life, for I have learned to exercise patience. If our ongoing relationship is to remain healthy, there is one piece of important information I must disclose to you. It is quite simple in nature and shared as a pet peeve by many. Considering I have met no one who enjoys being ignored by others, we probably share a common stance on the topic. I rarely favor repeating myself—if you never ask the same question twice, we shall continue playing nice.

You will find me different from most women in society; although I am excessively truthful, I've never been labeled by men as hormonally crazed, which is usually the title bestowed on women willing to speak their truth. I take that as a compliment since my brilliant word choice must confuse them so they cannot grasp that I am stating an opinion. Disclaimer spiel behind us, I will take the remainder of my breath from my breast to explain my process for judging the qualities of a person. When my swirling head finds a tendency utterly repulsive, my brain fixates on other heinous tendencies to justify my foul feelings. After I consolidate all the information, my mind can provide a trustworthy review. In all honesty, you should appreciate that I am willing to do the brunt of the work. While my brain completes exhausting gymnastic feats, you get to idly relax.

In all my spotty years of marriage, I've gone through my fair share of chambermaids, and in the short time I've had knowledge of Joseline's existence, she has been the most off-putting of the lot. You must understand I am generally very accommodating, and it is challenging for me to utter any words depicting my harsh criticism of the maid. Then again, I force myself to keep a judgmental eye. The world would be a better place if others could be as forthright as I am when bestowing assessments.

Before spouting a criticism, I try to give the individual the benefit of the doubt, often thinking of potential excuses that might justify their atrocious mannerisms. Believe me when I say the task has been difficult with Joseline. The only valid explanation I can muster for her inappropriate social behavior involves a narrative of her being orphaned as a child. Having no matriarchal figure around to give her guidance may have caused bearish tenancies to brew inside her. The possibility that the girl was abandoned is the only thing that gives me the required sympathy not to loathe her. I imagine she lives immersed in residual hurt. Giving myself the task of stepping into the role of her motherly figure, I match her stare to normalize her behavior. As soon as my eyes lock on hers, she squints back at me.

Is she trying to challenge me?

Did she not understand the essence of the polite gesture that shows my acceptance? I'm never the type to fold at a game of cards, I'm not ready to relinquish control. My eyes refrain from looking away. I would prefer my soul die before falling victim to an odd circumstantial defeat caused by unanswered questions. The idea of the child making a mockery of my life is unfathomable. Slightly closing the lids of my eyes, I reciprocate the intimidating squint, my foot tapping to distract my thoughts. Giving her another full minute, I find myself unable to entertain another second of her childish behavior and decide to speak. The sound of my throat clearing doesn't even cause her head to bobble, which sparks me to yell out my words like wildfire in her ears.

"I must ask a frivolous question, dear. Were you raised with parents as a child or orphaned?"

"I had a very normal upbringing, miss, with parents and all. Why do you ask?"

Her response is interesting. The degrading tonal quality of her words makes it difficult for me to maintain my composure, though, and I try to hide my grimace by tilting my head toward the floor.

"Fascinating. Isn't that just marvelous?" I say through clenched teeth.

She interprets my words as kudos, validating her perfect upbringing. An enormous smile accompanies her nodding head. I consider her response repulsive, making me want to dry heave. I'm not sure there's any possibility of her redeeming herself or making my opinion of her worse. In my mind, she's insufferably stuck in a pious purgatory.

"Yes, indeed, my childhood was quite nice," she states.

Her smirk gives me the blatant indication that her mind is lost in reminiscing thoughts of her picturesque upbringing. As I witness her teeter on a fine line of boastful bragging, I'm filled with anger.

Releasing a deep breath, I try to calm my ramping rage. "How wonderful for you that it was so perfect."

"Well, it wasn't all as it seemed, miss," she ventures.

Hearing this floods my mind with relief, and I can't help think of ways she could morph her subsequent words to redeem herself.

Is it possible she's been masking a tragedy, like childhood abuse?

"My parents were quite strict compared to others," Joseline says, her head lowered. "All my friends met up with the traveling soldiers when they visited our town, but I wasn't allowed."

Listening to what she considers a treacherous upbringing invites fits of rage to storm my veins. I can't believe she views her family's caring actions as abuse. She does not have the faintest idea of what it is like to grow up in a household of pure dysfunction and is clueless about living with parents who hate you more vehemently than if you were a mentally ill stranger. I find myself staring at her, unable to understand why the heavens gave her, and not me, a loving childhood. She, an ungrateful little twit, took the spot of a miserable child. She took the place of another small girl who would have killed to be have had a better home life, and that girl was me.

"Oh? That must have been terribly difficult for you," I say.

Her nose turns to the sky; I can tell right away my comment upset her.

"You have no idea," she replies.

She is the epitome of a spoiled brat. Clenching my fists, I try with all my might to fight away the blanket of anger the conversation had thrown upon me.

"Shall you run and fetch my shoes?" I ask her. "I dare say my feet are quite cold."

Swiftly Joseline turns around and dashes to the wardrobe to grab a pair of boots. During her departure, I try to distract myself. First, I gaze at my reflection, but it doesn't make me feel chipper like it usually does. Next, I tap my bare toe against the floor beneath my dress. As you undoubtedly are of intellect, you probably guessed my attempt to entertain myself has failed, leaving me to deal with each of my destructive emotions.

Why is she taking so long?

She is beyond infuriating. Each deep breath allows more oxygen to flow to my mind, and I think of all the ways my hands could kill her. As I clench my dress in my palms, my mind trails off with the thought of each hand wrapping around her neck. Slowly, as every finger tightens, I peer directly into her eyes. If she wants a staring contest, I will oblige, and it will be a game she'll never forget. Whom am I kidding? It will indeed be a game we both will never forget, and watching the light in her eyes diminish to a dull black will paint my soul in rainbow colors.

Imagine the rush I get from deciding when someone shall take their last breath; I dare say the feeling is irreplaceable. My knuckles squeeze harder, turning white. Joseline makes an effort to scream, but no sound comes out, and her mouth remains open, her tongue flailing. The organ's dancing movements and gasping sounds signal her fight for survival, each noise of suffocation resonating like an off-key horn in a royal court. Closing my eyes, I merrily hum along, and when I want more notes added to the melody, I spiritedly constrict my hands until the cartilage of her esophagus caves in.

My hands refuse to let go as her body falls limply to the floor. Traveling with her momentum causes my movement to mimic a drifting snowflake cascading to the ground. I watch my lethal hands morph into biting snakes, growing minds of their own. As they continue to crush her throat, the ongoing sensation of the crackling bone cools my anger. The need to peek at her lifeless face causes my eyes to leerily open. If anyone else were in a similar situation, surely they'd find happiness knowing the enemy they are battling is dead. The experience can only be compared to a militia fighting a yearlong war and finally witnessing its victorious results.

Just the thought of the image causes utter excitement to rush through my blood and a prickling sensation to tingle my skin. Allowing the anticipation to build makes me feel as though I'm receiving a gift for my behavior. Unable to take another exhilarating moment, I open my eyes the rest of the way. Although I expected to see Joseline's eyes glazed over with death, they regrettably appeared reanimated.

"Insufferable. You are insufferable! Why will you not die?" I shout.

Did I see things? Did her eyes blink? As I remove one hand from her throat, I analyze the damage I've inflicted. The severe bruising across her neck outlines the damaged cartilage through her delicate skin. Her lips are a light shade of purplish blue like a berry drained of color.

"Kill, kill, kill, kill," the voice chants from a distant corner of the room.

I recognize the tonal quality of the antagonizing words. While securing my hand to the girl's throat to stabilize her reanimating head, I tilt my skull to further investigate the resonating voice.

"Finish, finish, finish, finish," the voice bellows.

Seeing where the voice has led me, my eyes bring a warming smile across my lips. The sight of the dark corner engulfs me with familiarity and warmth. My friend is here; I knew I was not alone. Caught up in the moment of our reunion, I allow my eyelids to close and my ears to absorb each deep whisper. Refusing to end our moment of bonding causes me to delay dealing with the girl, and my hand further tightens.

"She's awake," the voice says, its breathy quality like that of a constricting serpent.

In unison with the words, I hear what sounds like a loud gasp near my hands. As I look down at Joseline's face, seething hatred fills my head. This ugly, despicable creature has ruined a cherished moment between my friend and me. Never can I forgive her. From the corner of my right eye, I see the shadow creep closer. The abrasiveness causes my cornea to become blinded by fits of spasms. Joseline's gaping mouth twitches as though it's trying to speak a trail of words, and I humbly laugh at the pathetic nature of her mannerisms. Each of my slight giggles provokes her bulging eyes to blink again.

This can't be happening.

Although I've read books that outline the potential for postmortem rehabilitation, I scarcely believed this was possible. Still, witnessing the maid's twitching facial features makes my confusion spiral, and glancing away, I take a second to clear my mind; I want a fresh set of eyes to analyze her abnormal movements. It feels like centuries pass as I take my time before looking back at her face.

"She has to be dead!" I say. At the same time, I look toward my friend, the shadow, for guidance.

Did I not see the light leave her eyes? That's the one thing I find tremendous enjoyment in, and if she were to take that away from me, I would be very disheartened.

"She's watching, watching, watching, watching you," the dark voice says, each word softer than the last.

Does she have no decency? Hearing my friend's warning of the one-woman audience makes the hinges of my jaw clench. Reluctantly I stare down at her annoying face and see something has shifted.

My mind races. *Is that a smile? Does she think I'm insane? She's the talking dead one, not me.*

Even in death, she thinks she is better than I. The smirk, plain as day on her face, proves the pretentiousness of her holier-than-thou mentality. Still fixated on her cracked lips, I glare as each corner continues to lengthen, and without an end in sight, her mouth shows both her top and bottom teeth as she cackles.

"Do you find me amusing?" I shout in her ear. "Am I a hilarious clown? You are the funny one, my dear. Just look at the tarnished appearance of your comically disfigured face. Your market value is now less than that of an aged prostitute, and the embarrassment you will bring to your family will cause your parents to discard you. They will wish you dead."

Upon the release of my last consonant, I swear the brat rolls her eyes at me in a dramatically condescending loop around the room. Believe me when I say her attitude would grate the nerves of even the most patient people.

"Finish, finish, finish, finish her," the voice urges.

I must finish the job I started, even though the blurred vision in my right eye is heightened with irritation. Tightening my grip, my hands turn into a wrench around

Joseline's fragile neck. The more the bone tears through the skin, the more her mocking laughter builds. Her mannerisms are both unstable and utterly insane. When she should be silent, she laughs, defying all living odds. She laughs, laughs, laughs, laughs. Her obnoxious cackle grows louder to provoke the sadistic thoughts that build in the temple of my mind. The influx of noise damages my skull as I reach my breaking point. Simultaneously, my shadowy friend applauds in the distance. The sinister encouragement brings me validation that I never was alone.

"Now!" the voice shouts.

The command triumphs over my feelings of anxiety. A moment later, the blurry sensation moves from my right eye to my left, causing me to panic. My jaw trembles and clenches at the thought that if I do not do my friend's bidding, my vision will be taken away as punishment.

"Kill!" the voice demands.

Without another thought, I cup each side of her ear canals, the flesh on her face radiating fire against my fingertips. Looking directly into the middle points of her eyes, I witness the whites surrounding her irises mirroring the color of flames. It was as if the fiery pits of hell encompassed me, providing a reflective backdrop to my ferocity-filled deeds. As rage overtakes me, my machine-like grip drives the back of her skull onto the hardwood floor. Blood spatters across my face with each whack, creating an ornate painting. The tepid substance warming my cold skin increases the momentum of my bludgeoning. Sounds of cracking bone echo throughout the room, and at that moment, I feel myself test a hypothesis: if she lives through this trauma, society will deem her a witch. The thought validates my actions.

Hitting her head harder against the floor, I imagine a crowd of villagers holding pitchforks and fiery torches, surrounding me to cheer on my victory. Letting their words guide my hands so I can give them what they want, I raise both hands to the ceiling, focusing as I aim toward her brow. Without warning, loud knocks resonate at the door. My mind and body freeze. My blurred vision quickly vanishes, and the light in the room appears brighter. Snapping my head to look toward the corner, I panic as I see the dissipation of darkness where the shadow was. Have I been caught? Nervously I clear my throat.

"Who is it?" I ask. Although my voice sounds shrill to my ears, it masks my inner panic well.

"It's your chambermaid, Joseline. May I come in to help you dress?" she replies.

The sound of the young girl's voice makes me shudder. Is it possible that even in death she still haunts me? My eyes graze the floor, and I realize the body is gone, and there is not one drop of blood on the wood. Did I imagine the whole thing? My mind can't help frantically running through what just occurred. My heart rate picks up, creating the escalating sensation of a panic attack. Cold sweeps over my bare skin. I notice I'm in my appropriate nightgown, and my eyes quickly scan the room. The sheets on the canopy bed appear slept in, and the despicable wedding dress hangs in the wardrobe.

"Just one moment!" I call.

As I jump up to my feet, my hands furiously rub my eyes to clear my vision. After swiftly moving back to my bed, I try to remain quiet as I climb under the covers and pull the top layer of sheets over my shoulders.

"You may come in now."

Hearing the ungreased hinges guide the door open triggers the first act of my performance. Keep in mind that I've been married multiple times, so this isn't the first time I've had to pretend to be sleeping. Watching Joseline take her first step into the room prompts me to yawn loudly and crack open my eyes.

"I must say, this bed has put a spell on me. I had the wildest assortment of dreams last night."

"All is good, I hope, miss. You sounded quite restless this morning," Joseline says, moving closer to the bed.

"Ah, yes. Each dream was very lavish and filled with merry tunes," I reply, hiding my uneasiness behind a disingenuous smile.

"Excellent, miss, as they should be because today is an exciting day!"

She shifts her trajectory to target each of the windows in the room and lets the morning light inside the four walls. She ties gold tapestry rope around the purple velvet as she opens each curtain. A smile falls on her face as she turns to look at me.

"I suppose it is," I reply, reluctantly mimicking her enthusiasm.

As Joseline's body approaches to help me out of bed, my mind drifts to the memory that depicts her pulverized skull. The sight of her pooling blood brought comfort to my day. Sniffing the air, I can still smell the tinges of the dry iron, and observing at the corner of the room gives me the clarity I need. Joseline peels the covers away from my shoulders and politely folds them at my feet. Releasing another fake yawn, I roll my body to the edge of the bed so my toes can touch the floor. The chambermaid's boot heels click loudly against the wood as she makes haste toward the hanging gown. Rummaging through the wardrobe, she searches for my undergarments and a pair of shoes.

"You're going to make the most beautiful bride," she says over her shoulder.

Bent over a pulled-out drawer, she continues to fetch items I will wear beneath the dress. I allow my total weight to transfer to my feet as I stand and prepare my torso for corseting by lifting my hands to the ceiling to stretch my spine. Lowering my hands back to my side, I walk toward the wardrobe.

"I dare say Mr. Fitz is one lucky man to be your husband," says Joseline. "Troves of suitors must have fought for that position."

As I attempt to contain my snicker, she grabs the last of my undergarments. Although the order of her execution is rather odd, I play up my naivete and let her start by putting the shoes on my feet. After tying the bows and finishing the final touches on each white lace boot, she spins and grabs the hanging corset. She places the heavy boning slightly over my bust and stations the bottom end over the upper portion of my hips. Slowly the air exits my chest. With each tightening pull, the capacity of my lungs becomes constricted and my head grows dizzy. With one last tug, my momentum shifts backward.

"I wish I could have a waist like yours, miss," Joseline says.

The last aggressive pull she gave my waist seemed oddly vindictive. Did she know of my dream? Or is she perhaps jealous? I've heard of societal men sticking their help, but I wouldn't think very highly of Mr. Fitz if that were his cup of tea, considering her appearance. Honestly, I would find it offensive if he chose me after her. Joseline moves her weight to the tips of her toes to take the dress from its hanging position. With a grunt, she embraces the entire body of the bulky lace gown with beaded detailing, and then she signals for me to step into the opened back. Her shaky hands can barely lift the heavy puffed sleeves over my shoulders. I watch as she struggles to clasp each hook and eye that line the back of the garment.

"Just beautiful," she says in a melancholy tone.

"You really must learn to control your emotions, Joseline, or you'll never attract a man," I scold her.

After timidly making their way to the front of the dress's skirt, her trembling hands fluff the petticoat. She lowers herself to the floor to fix nonexistent wrinkles in the material and distract her welling eyes.

"Good God, Joseline, you are going to stain this imported silk with your tears."

Placing my hands around her shoulders, I pretend to care about her escalating emotional state by helping her to her feet. Since I can remain honest with you, the actual reason I helped her is because it's an excellent manipulation tactic. I need her to like me if I'm to keep her as a confidant. An individual tear falls down her face, and she wipes it away with her sleeve. Sniffling, she moves behind me to remedy more wrinkles at the back of the dress. Thrown off guard, I feel the chain around my neck that holds the locket jostled. I abruptly turn to face her and swat her hand away from my neck.

"Don't you know what you're manhandling, child? This locket is the only memento that remains from my family before I was orphaned!"

"Mr. Fitz was very particular that you wear the jewelry he fetched for you," Joseline says, her hands retracting to her sides.

Who does this girl think she is? No one can tell me what to do. I glare into her eyes as though they are daggers stabbing her soul.

"Okay, miss. I apologize. I will let him know," the girl says, sheepishly lowering her eyes to the floor.

"Don't bother. I prefer to wait to disclose it until after the wedding is complete," I reply.

Her eyes mimic those of an abused puppy. If she wants to cheer me up for my big day, she'll need to adjust her attitude.

"Come on, girl. Brighten up," I urge her, a fake smile plastered across my face.

Tilting her head up to look at me causes her lips to break into a smile. She's becoming less emotional. I'm not one to complain, but her attitude is downright dreadful. I have enough on my mind, and I didn't need her malcontent nature bringing me down. If I'm to keep my mind sorted regarding facts, I need to have no other mental roadblocks holding me back. Grabbing my skirt with both hands, I dramatically fan the material and take a spin.

Joseline claps at my twirl. "Stunning, miss!"

Her encouraging words bring ammunition to my ego. As I continue my spin, I make eye contact with the standing vanity mirror across the room. Deciding I want to see my reflection, I pick up my speed. Before I realize it, I'm standing in front of the pristine glass, my hands smoothing out the crunched petticoat hidden beneath the silk of my dress.

"Beautiful," a deep voice chimes in from the corner.

In acknowledgment of the faint shadow in my line of sight, my head gives a slight nod. Joseline creeps up from behind me to get a better look at the dress's details.

"Do you fancy it?" I ask, pinching my cheeks to make them a rosy pink.

"Yes, miss. It is beautiful."

Taking not one moment of pause to analyze her expression, I continue to ogle my appearance in the mirror. "It shall be yours then. I have no need for it after the wedding."

Instantly she stops primping the ruffles of my dress, and with a shocked expression, she turns to look at me in the mirror.

"Oh, I couldn't," she replies hesitantly, shaking her head.

"Nonsense, child. I insist."

Her face, which was once in a melancholy state, instantly becomes joyful. I think she bought my kindness as genuine, and her enthusiasm to help me prepare for my wedding has grown. Each invigorated mannerism confirms I have her exactly where I want her.

"You don't know how much that means to me, miss. You truly are a godsend. A messenger notified me the police found my second cousin deceased this morning. Coming from a long line of chambermaids, she was also in the profession. It's just terrifying to think that could have been me."

Her clipped phrases sound like word vomit. Usually I pay little attention to statements made by the help, but this time is different. Her words trigger something inside me, and I can't help think back to my dream. My hands grow clammy as my stare freezes and my body tightens.

"Is everything okay, miss? You are as pale as a ghost."

Does she know what I've done? Was I careless with covering my tracks because I felt I had won with my invincibility? Quickly I try to mask my insecurities. Holding my breath, I attempt to speak.

"Anytime I hear the unsettling news that a child has died, my stomach becomes upset. Did they mention how the poor girl perished?"

"Of course, Miss. I am sorry to upset you. They found her frozen on the street. She was often tasked with running errands to town, and I guess she just didn't come back last night."

Feeling tremendously relieved by the news that my hands did not do the deed, I took a deep breath. Joseline comes across as confused by my response.

"Oh, child. Don't take my sigh as uncaring. I sighed at the relief that she went peacefully. Can you imagine if it had happened at the hand of one of her employers? There are mentally crazed people in the world, and it would sicken me even more than I already am if one of their hands disposed of her."

Joseline nods to show her understanding. "Don't worry. I heard nothing but great things about her employers. So that was never in question," she tries to assure me.

Immediately my mind eases. Sometimes I feel like my dreams border on reality, so I must be cautious of what information I relay. As I glimpse back in the mirror, I see my shoulders relax. "No more talk of sad things. Everything from now on will be joyous and happy."

"Yes, indeed, miss," Joseline replies.

I lock gazes with her and we both exchange smiles.

"You're truly the most stunning bride I've ever seen," she states.

"Thank you, sweet Joseline."

Controlling the sickening feelings buried deep inside my gut brings me a sense of comfort. The deep voice laughs from the room's corner; my friend is such a conniving devil, seeing through every lie.

"Shall we make our way to the carriage?" she asks.

I gesture in front of me. "Lead the way."

As I walk behind her and out of the room, I can't contain my smile. Compared to my fiancé's fate, the fact that I have to wear another white dress with frilly lace seems trivial to me. With each step, I enjoy every moment of this calm before the storm, and as I close the chamber door behind me, secretly I blow a kiss to the shadow.

Chapter Three

EAT MY WORDS

Making our way outside the estate is quite a deed for my poor little feet. One idea surrounding financial wealth I will never understand is why someone would pay to live in a maze. Some manors I have both lived in and seen are so monstrous they are obscene. Imagine waking up each morning knowing you spent much of your savings on an enormous dwelling that serves no purpose other than fortifying your ego and providing an array of rooms you'll never occupy. How many rooms does one need? Aside from a kitchen, sitting room, washroom, and bedroom, the rest is unnecessary fluff. In my humble opinion, all that extra stuff is a wasted investment. I can express an accurate assessment because I have been privileged to live in a bevy of lavish estates during my many marital adventures.

Let us take a moment and place ourselves in the excessive estate owner's shoes. Please close your eyes and picture yourself standing on top of an enormous mountain. As the wind blows through your hair, you smell slight hints of honeysuckle and pine. Though the scene appears relaxing, you notice a mysterious messenger bag perched on your shoulder. Curiosity overtaking you, you peek inside. The pack contains your entire life savings, along with a few scribbled loan documents from a local banker. You feel slightly confused by this odd placement of your cash.

In opposition to the peaceful scenery, you become anxious and wonder why your money isn't safely tucked away in the bank. As these thoughts engulf you, your hands become possessed and reach into the bag. Your eyes panic, and then your limbs become paralyzed as you witness each penny of your savings thrown to the wind by your disobedient hands, and the only thing you can do is wave at the money flying away. Now, stepping away from the scenario, let's put the concept into a larger perspective.

Let's pick up where we left off and start by asking a simple question. Now, if you believe my inquisition is obvious, do not laugh or shout your answer. It is always good practice to remember that what may be forthcoming to you may not always be that way for others. We must remain patient, even if another's mind seems filled with cobwebs. Here is the question: would throwing excessive amounts of money at nothing make you sick to the core? If you answered yes, you might find my next statement thought-provoking. The wealthy become so temperamental with prissy personalities because they are constantly concerned about losing the comfortable lifestyle to which they have grown accustomed.

I invite you to follow along as I hoist us a step further on our parallel discussion of thoughtful understanding regarding living the lonely life of unfulfilling choices. We are at the part of the philosophical lecture where I allow your hungry eyes to engulf a small secret. I should warn you: the notion I'm about to disclose will likely cause you to question your way of living and your views surrounding materialism.

Please take receipt of each word I am about to impart with caution. When someone purchases a home, their true inner colors reflect their selection. The favored architecture gives insight into someone's depth. From an estate's style, size, paint choice, artwork, or decoration, their inclinations expose each of their hidden qualities buried deep in their souls. I admire the beauty involved in purchasing something so dear to your heart.

Unfortunately, some take the sentiment for granted. Many are lured by materialism and strive only to live a life constructed around impressing others rather than simply delighting in the unique reflection they can offer to the world. The judgmental opinions of peers wash away each childhood dream regarding pursuits. Suppose their passion doesn't provide the necessary income to purchase, for example, an estate their peers will envy; in that case, they tailor their hopes and dreams on attaining the enviable asset. The individual willfully disregards their happiness and God-given talents to receive validation from others at the occasional dinner party. Living your life to please others is sad, exhausting, and lonely.

Sometimes I wonder if that is why the wealthy always have an atrociously sizable staff. With each additional person added to the roster, another lonely room will experience the sensation of a human footprint. The bulk of the house would continually lay dormant if the paid help no longer existed. Though it is not the accepted etiquette of the time, I would buy a home I find simplistic and easy to manage on my own. As much as a home speaks about someone's personality, it also can reveal their most profound insecurities. Unfortunately, I have learned the latter revelation from personal experience.

Through my years, I have gained a great deal of understanding about signifiers surrounding how others live. Each time I found it time to move into another fiancé's estate, my eyes grew smarter. After my first marriage, I learned to constantly scan my surroundings for embellishments that may act as grave warnings. I never entered into past relationships searching for the negatives, but rather something purposefully planted for me to find. Do not worry if you aren't tracking what I'm insinuating. Being privy to knowledge from books on the human mind is unnecessary; my passing of an understanding to you through storytelling will suffice, so let me tell you of the situation involving my first husband. He was a heinous man who does not deserve to have his first name repeated in conversation, so I will only mention it once. The devil's birth name was William. I will refer to him as husband number one and nothing more from here forward.

When my dear cousins in the nearby town graciously took me in as their ward, I became a creature others desired due to the novelty of my family's notorious demise. As I had little marital value in my parents' eyes, they felt it unnecessary to groom me in the intricacies of male relations. My naivete surrounding courting piqued the interest of my first husband. He was tall and lean. Something about the way a large slice of the whites of his eyes showed below his black iris' exuded sociopathy and triggered an uneasy feeling in my gut while in his presence. He acted as a confidante, but in actuality, he was a predator who capitalized on my insecurities. At first glance, I took his behavior as a bold gesture of kindness. Besides providing a listening ear, he often surprised me with flowers and decadent chocolates.

In all honesty, I should have taken the flowers as the first warning sign of his indifference because if he genuinely cared for me, he would have paid attention to what I enjoyed. He would have known I loathe flowers. Even something as small as that was a sign of his oppressive nature. Flowers do not interest me for many reasons. I view them as shrubs in disguise, like wolves in sheep's clothing. I do not need to bore you with the reason for my hatred, but I will reveal that it stems from my childhood.

Before he started giving them to me, he was already fully aware of my intense hatred of flowers. Together, we secretly mocked other suitors who bought them. It may seem harmless, but this was the first instance that he revealed his contradictions.

The relationship was a frantic whirlwind filled with many emotional trials, and our time together was wearing. The man always managed to be on his best behavior in public; he'd perform sweet gestures in front of others to maintain his reputation as a hero in the public eye, appearing like a savior sent to rescue me from my tragic childhood. Surprising me with gifts when I was shopping in town or having tea with an acquaintance was common. Surrendering to the whirlwind, I didn't ponder the question of how he knew where I was to deliver each trinket, and I naively turned a blind eye to his possible motives. Since I'd never been on the receiving end of doting behavior, I translated his actions as love rather than control. Reflecting on his tendencies, I find the sickest thing about the situation to be his explicit knowledge of what he was doing.

With every action, no matter how small, he was grooming me for a life of abuse. Trust me; I don't blame myself for falling victim to his persistent charm. I blame his putrid mind for capitalizing on my gullibility. When I agreed to be his fiancé, his behavior escalated to new heights, and I found myself shoved back into the shell I thought I had left behind in Northburry. After I accepted the ring, he made it clear I was his property and unapologetically dictated my every move. He constantly stated his likes and dislikes regarding my appearance, from my hairstyle to the color of my dress. How the public perceived me was of the utmost importance to him, as he held the opinions of those in his elitist social circles higher than my happiness.

It was abundantly clear he had lied when advertising himself as benign. He'd only used his comforting words as a manipulative tactic to draw me into his sociopathic vortex. Before our engagement, he often touted his differences from all other men, declaring he cherished a woman with intellect. He told me what I wanted to hear and knew the combination of words would bring me optimism. After catching him in his lies, I found him switching the narrative of both his and my words, and each time I softly queried his reliability, he vehemently questioned my sanity. Each passing day, he revealed tendencies of mine he despised, and eventually the emotional battery made me subservient. He challenged each unique quality I exhibited, including my love for reading. His psychological ownership over me made it emotionally impossible for me to break free and seeking his validation trapped me.

You may wonder what stopped me from leaving. The answer is simple: he viewed our relationship as a game of chess. Early in his courting, he made certain to befriend all who knew me. He planted seeds that painted him as a saint in their minds, so if we ever were to disagree, they would side with him. Wanting to ensure he remained the victim in any potential storyline made him obsessed with discrediting me and abolishing all negativity surrounding his image. Given how he portrayed himself as a decent man, his mistreatment perplexed me. In all reality, I was the victimized one. I was the prey in the twisted relationship, not him. The man was so narcissistic that he found it acceptable to claim my truth, and I hated him for that.

Repeatedly he forced me to listen to his same conversation. To each new person we met, he'd advertise himself as a generous protector of others. That alone should have had me running the opposite way, but the thought of the dangerous repercussions stopped me. I will share with you a valuable lesson I have learned: if a person is genuinely kind to their core, they will not boastfully detail each reason you should believe it to be true.

Some extreme contradictions I found within his falsehoods included severe bouts of screaming and constant twisting of the words I had shared with him in my most vulnerable moments. There was a split second when I assumed his bark might be more significant than his bite. That brief moment of courage caused me to be reckless several days before our wedding and I tried to run. For those of you who think I was a coward, you are wrong. Even in my beaten-down shell, I am resilient. Repeating the same steps I took to escape my family home, I crept out at night to find transportation in the center of town. I did not consider that, unlike the last time, I was recognizable. I'd let the fact that our engagement had been posted in the local paper slip through my mind.

As I stepped into the carriage, the man steering the reins realized my identity. Can you believe the individual dared to return me to my fiancé's estate upon his discovery? Well, he did. Immediately upon entering the estate's front door, I slipped up to my private quarters to prepare for bed. The driver let himself in and proceeded to fill my fiancé in on my whereabouts. Trust me, he wasn't happy to have been woken by my late return. Noiselessly he lingered outside my bedroom door while I undressed—the most patient I'd ever seen him. Once I was fully unclothed, he threw open my chamber door and made his embarrassment known at my most vulnerable moment. He took his anger out by viciously beating me and bestowing a multitude of merciless lashes on my back. The castigation was severe.

When we woke up the following day, he pretended to be a gentleman and called the seamstress to alter the wedding dress to hide my bruised spine. Because of his status, everyone turned a blind eye to the evidence that blatantly stained my skin. He blamed my rebellion for triggering his outlandish spurt of anger. Please refrain from giving me looks of pity; I know the situation was wretched. I didn't even allow myself to know pity. Instead of wallowing in misery, I turned my anguish into deep-seated hatred. After that treacherous night, a mysterious hunger/pain stemmed from the pit of my stomach and rage fed it. Leading up to the infamous day, I found that the ache became more unbearable every time I peered into his eyes. What is the infamous day, you ask? Well, of course, it is the day of his death. Don't worry; I didn't let him live long. I made sure he took his last breath shortly after our ceremony ended.

Honestly, the recurring dream of seeing my deceased family sitting around the dining table was a tremendous blessing, as each of the gruesome details numbed any potential squeamish feelings I might have been carrying inside. I am thankful for having no fear surrounding the sight of blood. Their hacked bodies were, dare I say, inspirational to me.

When husband number one and I arrived home after the wedding, I noticed his anger. Immediately my thoughts centered around surviving the night unscathed, as well as selecting a new book from the study.

We had come to a happy compromise to keep our marriage on livable terms. We agreed that if I were to perform to his standards every day, he would reward my compliance by allowing me to read another book. The wedding day concluded without him verbally berating me. I believed it was apparent he was content with my behavior, and he would allow me my prize in exchange for my compliance.

My feet picked up their pace and crossed the foyer before I heard the front door close behind me. There was no welcome from the waitstaff since all had been given the night off because of the celebration. The only thing on my mind was how quickly I might escape in the literature I was about to devour. Each leather-bound novel acted as the only form of happiness I had remaining. Fixated by the excitement surrounding every book, I forgot all about the uncomfortableness of my wedding gown and undergarments. Making my way down the marble-tiled hallway, I saw the library door was open and ran faster. As I stood in the room, a sense of calm fell over my body.

The smell of the musty books provided the necessary oxygen for my lungs to breathe. I raced to the nearest shelf, closed my eyes, and thumbed through the rows of bound spines. Slowly I traced the ridges of each textured back until my sightless touch settled on a final choice. My engrossment in my blind selection of new reading material distracted my mind and made my ears complacent to the heavy footsteps coming from behind.

"What do you think you're doing, girl?" husband number one roared.

The sound of his booming voice made my eyes spring open, lungs gasp, and fingers pause. Still permitting my finger to caress the spine of the comforting vintage book, I tried to slow the pace of my heart. Taking a moment, I languidly pivoted my torso to look in his direction, but then I quickly averted my gaze to the floor. Each of my body's movements felt like a deranged chore.

"I-I-I thought I was good today," I replied.

"Was the reward of a wedding not enough?"

"It was—" I said, wrapping my hand tighter around the book.

Before I could finish, he cleared his throat and aggressively ran toward me. Swiftly I pulled the book from the shelf and shifted my body to the side to dodge his rage-filled onslaught. Each time I was offered champagne at the wedding, I secretly tossed the drink under the table. I knew my coherence was imperative if I were to deal with him later. Unlike me, he finished every glass to celebrate the occasion, and his intoxication showed. My eyes widened as the sound of his blundering body crashing into the wooden shelves echoed throughout the cavernous room. Watching him tumble to the floor warmed my body with excitement. With each of my wicked thoughts, the room darkened.

"Kill him," said the shadow.

The sound of the voice made my eyes dart to the shadows. My familiar friend was nearby to comfort me, filling my heart cavity with warmth and causing my right eye to twitch.

"Kill!" the voice screeched.

My grip clenched tighter around the book's leather as the voice's volume grew voluptuously near my ears. Still stunned by the fall, husband number one angrily glared up at the assaulting bookshelves and gawped in horror as they swayed back and forth, back and forth. Realizing his precarious situation, he raised his arms to shield his head from the teetering shelves filled with skull-plundering literature. Suddenly, with excellent synchronization, all but one bookcase topples, crushing him. It was almost as if they had planned the attack to free me from the shackles of his control. They bore witness to the horrible words he uttered and beatings he served. The only explanation I constructed for how each of the books fell in unison was that it was an act of camaraderie. As he lay pinned, his eyes flashed to the top shelf of the last standing bookcase just in time to see a final book abandon its wooden platform. The book's extensive contents built an incredible velocity as the volume hurled through the air. He couldn't react in time, and I watched gleefully as the large object bludgeoned his skull.

"Finish him," the voice commanded, the demanding words emanating from the room's darkest corner.

His breathing sounded like an annoying fireplace bellows as he struggled to gather a lungful of air under the weight of the shelves and literature. Gurgling sounds stemmed from his lungs, and the consistent garble made me believe he had fluid in his esophagus. Streams of blood rolled down his face like rainfall down a mountain's peak. Each drop traveled from the open wounds on top of his head and down his nose. As there was so much blood, it was difficult to decipher which injury contributed the most to the glorious red river, but I was almost certain the last bash of his head had caused him to descend into his vegetable state. His limbs did not indicate future movement as he limply lay on the floor. Books and a pool of blood seeping into each cover surrounded his body. The scene sparked feelings of disbelief. How was it possible? Even in death, he had ruined classic literature. The aching pit in my stomach grew as I observed his bodily fluids stain the integrity of the toppled books. I can safely say his outlandish repulsiveness irritated me greatly.

"No! They did nothing to deserve such treatment," I cried.

I set the book in my hand on a nearby desk for safekeeping, then sprinted across the room to rescue the drowning books.

"He's a beast," my friend said.

Hearing the voice made me race faster. I paused a few inches from the grotesque image and admired the most significant book on the floor. It was the last book to fall and thrash the man's skull. Upon closer examination, I realized it was the atlas I had smuggled with me from Northburry. The fact that the ornate cover had avoided each drop of fluid made me laugh. The dreadful sounds of his coughing corpse dismissed the peace, and with every hack, he spewed more blood like a cheap fountain. If I were to save these books, I had to act in haste. As I was greatly indebted to the precious atlas, it was imperative I save it first. It was second nature for me to target the treasured book before the rest and protect it before becoming engulfed by the thrill of the mission.

Paying no attention to the impractical dress that still clung to my body, I tripped over the bulky skirt. The momentum from my sprint propelled my body as it hit the floor. After uncontrollably sliding across the hardwood planking, I landed in a stagnant pool of blood. The sight of my white dress soaking up the red substance like a sponge made me think back to my recurring dream. I couldn't help wonder if this was a sign that it was time to commence my shadow friend's mission. The burgundy puddle eerily reminded me of the red wine I had spilled on Daniel's floor, and everything turned full circle. Closing my eyes, I allowed my nostrils to take in the pungent smell of damp iron, and the scent overcame me with serenity.

Sounds of raspy breathing cut through the silence, ruining my peaceful concentration. Reluctantly I turned my head to look in the noise's direction.

"Oh, I almost forgot you were there," I said.

Upon ending my statement, I swear I heard the shadow laugh from the corner, and I joined in. As husband one released a loud hacking noise to clear the blood from his throat, I paused my giggling to listen. His coughing sounded like he was joining in our laughter. My knees wriggle through the pool of blood and make their way to his shoulders for a confrontation.

"Do you find this funny?" I asked.

As he swam in and out of consciousness, his incoherent eyes rolled back in his head. I wanted to be in control and his lack of listening limited my experience. Why had my mood not improved? Was it not enough to watch the light leave his eyes? I took a moment to sort out my confusion.

"Will you feel relieved when his breath ceases?" my friend asked.

Turning to investigate the shadow, I heard my new husband's frantic breathing crescendo. The obnoxious exhalations created an annoying echo in the room, the noise defragmenting my detailed thoughts.

"Coward," my first husband muttered.

My head snapped in his direction. *Did he just speak?*

"What did you say?" I asked.

I waited for him to repeat himself, but he expelled blood rather than words. He was insufferable.

Instead of using his last breaths to call for help, he would rather belittle me?

My flesh turned red with thoughts of the many times he had mistreated me. I clenched my fists in an attempt to subdue my anger. Usually I found it easy to hold my tongue, but this time was different. Though I couldn't stop shaking, my mind remained in control. I wiped my hands clean on my wedding dress to provide my fingers with better gripping power, and then I furiously snatched up the atlas.

"Who's the coward now?" I said.

The reflection of the book becoming larger in his pupils brought irreplaceable satisfaction to my frenzy. Honestly, it might have been one of my most cherished moments. As his eyes gave one last widening plea, the rage in my fingertips became one with the atlas, and I used every ounce of my might to bash the heavy book against his mangled face and crush his skull.

"Whack, whack, whack, whack," the shadow repeated with each bludgeoning blow.

"Whack, whack, whack, whack," I responded as each strike hit its mark.

Carried away by the exhilarating power running through my veins, I lost track of how many times I hit the man. With the sound of cracking bone, I chuckled, and my hands stopped to assess the state of his face. He looked revolting. For once in his life, his outer appearance reflected the contents of his soul.

"Oh, dear me! What will your gentlemen's club think of your new exterior?" I said.

Something shocking met my ears as I leaned over his face to check for life. He was still breathing, and though the sound was hushed, it baffled me.

How is he still living?

I couldn't fathom by what means his unintelligible features could function adequately enough to gather oxygen.

"Finish the creature," the shadow commanded.

I knew my friend was right. Even though husband number one had treated me dreadfully, I couldn't leave him to suffer in his misery. That would be cruel, and I would never stoop to his level of barbarity. Staring at the book in my hand made my thoughts run wild, and I couldn't help remember every time he made me feel inferior. Quite frankly, my intelligence and education exceeded his, and he was aware of that. I often believed the reason he belittled me was due to his fear of my intellect. As I raised the book to the ceiling, a brilliant idea came to mind, and my lips twitched with a smile. The next part didn't cause me turmoil as some may assume. Acknowledging the book would serve a grand purpose, I easily tore out each page. Using a single hand, I pried open his mouth. As I crumpled the pages into a wad, I forcefully lodged them down the back of his throat until his mouth reached its capacity.

"Now you truly know what it's like to be engulfed by a well-written novel," I said.

My grin grew as I listened to his beating heart stop. He could no longer hurt me or anyone else—I was free. All at once, the severity of the situation set in. As my eyes slowly panned the gruesome scene, the massive bloody stains on my wedding gown caught my attention.

"What will people think?" I said.

The last thing I wanted to take the blame for was a fool's demise. Having read many mystery novels, I knew I had two options: 1) I could run, or 2) I could play the victim card. While I was married to my departed husband, I learned a great deal about manipulation. A chilling rush through my core signaled the shadow was reaching out to help. My friend had planted an idea in my mind regarding how I would escape. If I were to continue to do my friend's bidding, it was imperative not to get caught, so for that reason, I know I must listen. The rattling of the top desk drawer piqued my curiosity. After getting to my feet, I walked over to investigate the haunted drawer. When I pulled it open and looked inside, I was pleased to find financial reports as well as envelopes filled with money.

My thoughtful friend had provided me with the means for both my travel and survival. I knew if I were to stage the scene as a robbery, no one would expect me to be the culprit, and I could start over in a new city under a different name. The thought of seeing a new place brought excitement to my bones.

How am I to make this believable?

If a serial criminal committed this atrocity, he would have a pattern when executing the assault and leave a trademark. Eureka! I indeed would have to ditch the blood-soaked wedding gown, so why not use it to help paint a picture for the discovery? Searching the other drawers, I found a pair of scissors and hastily cut the dress from my body. Once unclothed, I used the blades to shred the material, giving the impression someone had violently torn the gown from my fragile frame. I then covered the fabric in blood to make it appear as though I, too, had been a casualty of the violent invasion. I shredded each layer of my dead husband's clothing to mimic my feigned attack. After cutting the items from his body, I tossed the heap of bloody clothing into a corner of the room. To assure no fingers were pointed at me, it needed to appear that we both had fallen victim to the crime. Realistically, the authorities would be so overwhelmed by the details of the perfectly staged scene that they'd likely assume the brutish intruders had kidnapped and killed me.

Carefully I added my shoes to the heap of evidence and wiped my hands on an untainted piece of fabric in the pile of clothes. Avoiding stepping in the blood, I ran back to the open drawer to take the cash-filled envelopes and picked up the book I had set down earlier for safekeeping; I'd need material to read during my lengthy travels. While exiting, I kicked over a few furniture items to complete the illusion of a struggle. I suspect they would stop searching for me after a couple of weeks and shortly thereafter pronounce me deceased. My shadowy friend's smile confirmed the plan was foolproof.

Hastily I went upstairs and found an old dress I determined no one would notice if taken from my closet. Since my body would be missing, my quarters would be one of the first places investigated, so nothing of basic necessity could be removed. I took several pieces of jewelry with me, including my unique locket. Don't judge me. It was something a robber would take, and I wanted to preserve an accurate storyline. If I seized more than that, it might raise suspicion that I had packed up my life and run. Leaving my luggage behind felt like a new beginning. All I had was the book in my hand and the rightfully deserved inheritance tucked into my bosom.

Exiting the front door of the estate, I felt invincible. I didn't look back and left the door wide open. With the shadow's help, I found fleeing Hillstead incredibly easy. The events gave my life purpose, and from that day forward, I made it my mission to be a vigilante. I put all my trust in the shadow's advice and relished in the fact that I would rid the world of vile misogynistic rubbish. Marriage is a ghastly one-sided act, and though no one was willing to help me, I will advocate for the meek and prevent the suffering of other young women.

The bottoms of my feet grew tired as I walked until sunset. When I arrived at the last shadowy corner of my journey, a dark carriage led by a single black stallion pulled up beside me, and the driver called down to ask if I would like a ride. He was an older man who reeked of piss and whiskey, but he didn't seem to recognize my face, so I climbed inside and took a seat. Within moments my lids closed and the swaying carriage rocked me to sleep. When I awoke, we had traveled for at least a day. I pushed back the small curtain and gazed through the window at the unfamiliar surroundings. The horse came to a halt in a town I didn't recognize.

"This is your stop, miss," the driver said over his shoulder.

"Perfect," I said, still gazing out the window.

My normal breathing resumed as I stepped into the street of the quaint town. I had escaped. When I turned to ask the driver how much I owed him, the carriage no longer was there. Although its silent departure was odd, it was the least of my concerns. What was of the utmost importance was that I was free to build a new life in this little town called Bickerton.

With my cash in hand, I promptly settled into a quiet cottage and made it a daily ritual to sit with a cup of tea and read the local paper. One morning, while sitting in a nearby café, I came across an article describing the elaborate robbery at husband number one's estate, and I couldn't help snicker. I was one clever fox. Since they had no pictures to identify me, they had hired an unskilled caricature artist to re-create a likeness that bore no similarity to mine.

Well, would you look at that? Our timing is supreme. The story is finished, and it appears we are nearing the front entrance of husband number five's estate. Passing through the final Grecian-styled marble corridor, we finally arrive at the foyer. Joseline dashes ahead of me and uses both hands to push open the massive French doors.

"This way, miss," she says.

I smile at her as I walk through, shielding my eyes from the sun. Quickly she grabs the bottom of my dress to lift it from the ground and ushers me to an ivory carriage with white horses.

Can you get any more cliche? For me, this is the furthest experience from a fairy tale.

If this is what I have to deal with, masking my annoyance for the entire day will be a grand feat. Joseline finishes helping me into the coach's cabin then climbs in after me. The sound of the door closing confirms we are off to the races.

Yippee. I need a drink.

Chapter Four
LET'S GO FOX HUNTING

The horses' hooves sound like toasting champagne glasses as they strike the cobblestone path. Each trot brings growing resentment from the carriage wheels as they must tread along the uneven texture of the jagged stone. It is turbulent, to say the least, and I can't help wonder if the driver is trying to ruffle us up on purpose. A slight bump in the terrain makes my body airborne. The jarring movement triggers my hands' frantic gripping of the upholstered bench underneath me.

"The ride will get better, miss," Joseline says. "I promise we only have until the bridge, and then it will be smooth."

Her attempt to divert her anxiety to me is absurd. I force a grin on my lips to cover up my annoyance over our bumpy ride. Silently nodding, I peer out the window to gauge the distance we have left until the bridge, and my eyes fixate on the rocky man-made stream that flows underneath. My pupils follow the moving water, which leads to a large fishing hole. So your eyes can paint a better picture of what I'm witnessing, I will provide you with the best aesthetic comparison I can. The scenery outside has a similar appeal to what many would call the French countryside. Every rock laid on the bridge has tiny grass sprouts trying to escape between each aged joint. The wind blows through the green field surrounding the willow trees as small yellow flowers interlace clusters of healthy grass. The prior rainfall left every stone on the bridge dark, and its age shows through its wear.

"You need some fresh air," Joseline says.

Do I appear sick?

Her skin displays a tinge of green, not mine. As I hold my tongue, she flounders. That my silence makes her uncomfortable brings me enjoyment. Swiftly her fingers scramble with the small window's crank to crack the glass open. As soon as she lets fresh air inside the cabin, her face takes on a natural shade.

"Are you better, child?" I ask.

Nervously she nods as she seals the window. Feeling better, she sits back on the bench across from me, releasing a dramatic exhalation.

"I just wanted to make sure you're comfortable. I'm never queasy, but this confinement is a bit suffocating. Did the air help you, miss?" she asks.

Why is this child still rambling? Does she not realize how easy it is to read her fraudulent facial expressions? She soon will be in for a rude awakening if she thinks she can outsmart me. She's fortunate I'm attempting to save energy by postponing my lecture to her. Since it won't be beneficial at this moment, I will spare both of us the wasted time. I need to conserve as much wit as possible before the looming series of events commences.

"Indeed," I reply.

She interprets my response as a compliment. The thought of her being the reason for my good health forms a proud smile on her face. Out of courtesy, I give a half-smile back just as the carriage encounters a bump. Her body jolts from the turbulent movement, and my grip on the seat tightens.

"We must be crossing the bridge," Joseline says.

Beneath us, the sound of running water grows louder and complements each horse's neighs. The sound prompts me to peer out the window at the creek. An uneasy sensation falls over my heart, causing me to reach for the locket around my neck. The scenery has triggered a peculiar response in me, and I take a deep breath. The metal's cold temperature calms my racing mind and brings me security. Sometimes my memories mesh together, and I'm relieved not to remember all the details.

If I can escape the triggered memories, I can hide my emotional scars very well. Over time, boxing away each emotional episode has become more burdensome. Certain things in my present life often prompt memories involving my past killings that provoke my mind to spiral. With my head pressed against the carriage wall, I shift and peer out the window. I need to calm my panicked mind by pinpointing the trigger point that haunts me.

Why is this view torturing me?

"The beauty of the scenery can make me emotional too. It reminds me of my childhood. Is it the same for you, miss?" Joseline says, probably in an attempt to distract herself from her nausea.

I gulp as my eyes remain fixed on the scenery outside. Joseline isn't well versed in reading others' emotional cues, and I sense something must be wrong with her. The child needs to understand when it is appropriate to talk. If I weren't so focused on trying to place the vague familiarity of the countryside, I would be more than eager to shed some light on her lack of social etiquette. The sound of the carriage's wheels adds to the nostalgia that plagues my thoughts. As I squeeze my eyelids shut, I allow the flooding memories to take over my imagination. Upon opening my eyes, I find Joseline has vanished, and in her stead sits my giant bear of a second husband, staring back at me with his amber-brown eyes and perfectly quaffed cocoa-colored locks.

My mouth wasn't planning to speak about his story, but since he has made an uninvited appearance, I will take a moment to tell you about him and what transpired between us during our brief year or so relationship. As with my discussion of my first husband, I will refrain from using his name more than once. I must disclose something I believe you may already perceive. Like the others, I hated my second husband, John, but the wonderful thing about this relationship compared to the others was our mutual loathing. We despised each other, and given his overly boisterous personality, he wasn't shy about showing it.

Another aspect I found thought-provoking was his unusual personality. Although his estate was grand, he preferred to stay in his country cottage, especially when he had the urge to hunt. There was something especially peculiar about how much he enjoyed prowling for animals. Although men generally possess more animalistic characteristics than women—some will hunt to provide food for their family—husband number two was different.

He enjoyed hunting because it offered him the opportunity to torture defenseless creatures without being questioned.

The scenic familiarity I find in the countryside makes perfect sense since the acreage surrounding husband number twos' estate was similar to the backdrop passing by my window. I don't make a peep as I stare into his green flecked pupils. The sight of his lips cracking a smirk sends jitters down my spine. It's the same unnerving grin he had plastered on his face when he perished. Even in postmortem, the eerie grin remains etched on his lips, as if he's pleased about dying.

You may assume my relationship with husband number two was toxic, and I can assure you it was. Next, you may wonder how two individuals like us met, and I will tell you it was nothing like how I met my first husband. I sought to marry husband number two for his extraordinary personality. The storyline picks up shortly after I moved into my cottage. When I was sipping tea at the café, perusing a newspaper article detailing my staged robbery, he appeared. The man entered the cafe like clockwork. Slowly I lowered the newspaper to uncover my face, and we locked eyes and exchanged a grin. At first glance, I noted his visibly appealing nature; subsequently, his awful personality came as no surprise. To gather evidence for my discernment, I intently scrutinized how he treated others from behind the printed papyrus. His impatience escalated moments after he placed an order for his tea, his belligerent demands intensifying after only ten minutes of waiting. His innocent waitress darted to his table in an attempt to alleviate his concerns. She was an agreeable young female with a seamless adolescent updo. Her dress was nondescript with gray and white tones.

Since she isn't a focal point of the information you yearn for, I won't bombard you with needless descriptions.

Although his behavior should come as no surprise, even I was taken aback by his subsequent actions. When the young woman failed at her mission, she turned to retreat to the front counter, and he slapped her backside. As I watched his disgusting behavior unfold, it took everything in me not to cause a scene and spoil my mission. Deep in my gut, if he acted this way in public, I knew greater demons resided behind closed doors. Therefore, I would need to emulate the floozy he desired in order to pique his interest. Attempting to do something I'd never done before, I obnoxiously giggled and batted my eyelashes. My attempt to catch his attention provoked his curiosity. In all honesty, my performance was immaculate, and I wasn't surprised he fell for my theatrics. As he slowly approached my seat, he resembled a panther hunting its next victim.

"Good afternoon, miss," he began. "From across the room, I noticed you were unaccompanied, and being a true gentleman, I had to introduce myself. I would rather die than not fulfill my gentlemanly duty of offering my company to such a beautiful young lady."

I observed him lower the brim of his felt hat to lessen his intimidation. It's an overdone move many men perform--- to manipulate women during the early stages of courting. The only thing missing from this cliché scene was a single rose to sweep me off my feet. His perfectly straight teeth and sadistic smile told me all I needed to know: he could swoon any woman of his choosing, and I had to stop him from taking advantage of that. Noticing my lack of response to his advance made him anxiously perplexed.

"Oh, silly me," he said. "Based on how I just acted, you'd never guess my mother properly raised me.".

I remained silent to observe what he would do next. Raising his fist to the sky, he abrasively snaps his fingers to get the poor server's attention. The young girl at the counter dropped what she was doing and frantically headed to our table.

"Yes, sir," she said.

Her fear was so blatant you could smell it on her scurrying petticoat. Obviously, this was a regular interaction for them and not the first occurrence of the man's disrespectful behavior toward her. She couldn't even look him in the eyes.

"Aw, yes. Do you have flowers? A lady as stunning as..." he said, fishing for my name.

"Beatrice. My name is Beatrice," I said.

Hearing the name made his eyes light up with excitement. It came as no surprise to him that he'd easily gotten what he wanted. He threw his hands in the air, continuing to make a striking scene with his theatrics.

"Have you ever heard of a more enchanting name?" he asked.

The child flinched as she glanced back to a flower advertisement on a bare countertop. By her nervous behavior, I could tell something was wrong. His hand dived into his coin pouch and removed a few shillings.

"We don't have flowers, sir," she said with apprehension.

The sound of her fast words made his body freeze and his jaw clench.

"What?"

"Our delivery is late today, so they haven't come in yet."

Her explanation didn't help defuse his festering anger. It did the opposite, and he silently glared at her until her body trembled. Once he knew the fear had made her submissive, he lightly cleared his throat to see if she would jump. Of course, she did what he expected, and he found enjoyment in the feeling of control. After rummaging a bit more through his coin pouch, he retrieved a few additional coins to extend to her.

"I'll tell you what, girl. I'll let this situation slide if you take these and fetch a beautiful bouquet from the square for Beatrice. What do you say? Do we have a deal? You—" he said through gritted teeth.

Before he could finish the solicitation, she cautiously grabbed the money with a shaky hand and nodded. His controlling mannerisms continued as he turned his body to stare at her as she exited. As soon as the bell jingled, signaling the door had shut, he redirected his attention to me. He aggressively sat down in the seat beside me with a pompous attitude. The fact that he didn't even ask if I liked flowers was enough to signal that he grouped all women into the same category. He glanced at the newspaper in the middle of the small round table. Following his line of sight, I saw the page still turned to the article about my crime, and I panicked.

Will he realize it's me? Is this where I get caught?

Pretending to be harmless, I let my eyes gaze at my teacup to alleviate any suspicion. After snatching the paper up from the table, he held it in front of me, forcing me to stare at the photo accompanying the article.

"Don't tell me you read," he said, his body shaking with rolling laughter.

I obnoxiously giggle to mask my disdain. "Do I read? Oh, God, no, sir. That is a valueless activity for a woman. No affluent lady should ever waste her time on such frivolity. I would rather perish than be bored by printed words."

"So why is this on the table, then?"

As I leaned toward him, I pushed my bust together with my elbows and pointed to the cartoonish drawing of myself. As expected, his eyes never left my chest.

"The drawings are just so magnificent," I said. "Sometimes, I find my feminine brain unable to look away."

Honestly, at that point, it was apparent he wasn't paying attention to anything coming from my mouth. I probably could have disclosed I had performed the whole murderous scene plus escaped, and he wouldn't have flinched. Instead of listening, he grossly bit his lip as he fantasized about my cleavage.

"That's just perfect," he murmured.

He was a loathsome cave dweller with no taste. The bell on the shop's front door jingled, its echo knocking him out of his daydream. Reluctantly he turned toward the small girl carrying an enormous bouquet of colorful flowers to the table. Before she could even come to a stop to hand him the arrangement, he aggressively snatched them from her cradled grip.

"Beautiful flowers for a beautiful creature," he stated.

Disgusting. This little charade cannot possibly be working for him.

I tried to force a coy smile on my lips. Considering each of the cut flowers smelled of ghastly fragrances, I found it hard to ignore my watering eyes. As I've mentioned, I hate flowers. Earlier I had told you I would refrain from forcing the details upon your mind, but since it seems to be a recurring problem within all my marriages, I will take the time to explain why I despise the vile things.

When a florist composes an arrangement, such as the one I was forced to regard, I can't help fixating on the flowers' mutilated stems. Staring at a vase of flowers is like gaping at a corpse at an open-casket funeral. We ruin picture-perfect beauty for our frivolous pleasure by beheading each flowering creature and thoughtlessly placing the carnage on display. Humans aren't satisfied cherishing natural beauty; instead they feel a need to pillage to possess it for themselves. It is perplexing why one would not just plant a rose bush to admire from a home's window. Unfortunately, many feel it is justified to forcefully kidnap the blooms from their habitat for the sole purpose of satisfying their visual pleasure. The most despicable motive for a flower's early demise is its nonconsenting use in fraudulent acts of contrition. Typically men present flowers as an apology in a relationship, with the intent that the fragrant bright-colored petals will erase their wrongs and put loved ones back in a splendid mood. Have we ever thought perhaps the perpetrator should choose to refrain from being loathsome in the first place? If they treated us less with less ill will, I dare say it would save the lives of a lot of flowers. In my eyes, it would be a societal victory.

This task may be difficult for some, but entertain me by thinking back to each of your past relationship conflicts. I challenge you to dissect the reason you forgave your significant other. When they walked through the front door to finally face the aftermath of their undesirable behavior, did they truly mean the apology? Did the heartache they caused within you dissipate with the sight of dead flowers? Most of the time, we forgive the wolf superficially because we know what's expected from us when we receive a gift. Once we declare their gesture acceptable, the suitor learns that the cyclic pattern is tolerated, and they're free to do as they wish with very little consequence. Masking their cruelty behind the gift of simple shrubs allows them to deem themselves invincible. I use the word "shrubs" because a flower's beauty should not be associated with the cycle of emotional abuse.

As a small child, I witnessed my father perform the vile act with my mother. Each time he squandered our household money on gambling or liquor, he emerged with an obscene bouquet to apologize. The roses did nothing to repair the woman's suppressed anger and only contributed to her bitterness and low self-esteem. Regardless of the number of redundant words and ornate arrangements, his inexcusable behavior remained steadfast except on the fleeting occasion when he ran out of money to feed his vices. Over time, the more shrubs my mother was given, the more her resentment grew toward her life and family. Even though my father's apologies didn't hold an ounce of validity, they further lost their meaning when presented with monetary strings. I detest apologies; they are strictly for fools. If you genuinely have remorse for your behavior, change your actions. Better yet, avoid performing the despicable act in the first place. It is so simple, yet society thrives off grand gestures and focuses too much on buying forgiveness to mend our wrongdoings rather than correcting the root cause.

As he held the bulky shrubs in front of my eyes, I seized my breath in an effort not to sneeze. Impatient with me for not taking hold of the stems, he waved the arrangement in my face.

Does he not think I can see them?

With a smile cracking across my lips, I reluctantly grasped the bouquet. "Thank you. They are lovely," I stated.

I saw the smug expression on his face and flirtatiously winking eye as I lowered the arrangement to the table. To divert my desire to dry heave, I turned to face the server, who remained next to the table.

"You did an excellent job selecting these," I said.

"Thank you, miss," she replied.

Judging from her smile, my compliment meant a lot to her, and her reaction made me happy. Taking her newfound glee, she turned around and returned to the counter. Once again, the gentleman and I were alone with nothing in common.

"I think you and I have a lot in common," he said.

Compulsively I chuckled. "Oh, really?"

"I like how we can have these deep conversations. Mark my words: today was destiny, and we will marry," he stated arrogantly.

Pleased my plan was a success so far, I silently gazed into his eyes to allow him to revel in his moment of boastful pleasure over the prize he had won.

After releasing an imposing exhalation, he commandingly stood up and paused. "Silence is bliss, Beatrice. It's like you already know me so well," he said.

He was accurate when he said I knew him well. Though his general impression was correct, my familiarity with him didn't come from what he thought. My knowledge of him didn't stem from the topics of our conversation but rather his choice of words and actions. I knew him well because he was narcissistic, and I recognized each idiosyncrasy believed to accompany the psychosis. His face glowed with happiness as he left the café.

As I scanned the far corner of the room, I spotted a single chair resting in the shadow. "No time to rest. I guarantee the second shall be the best," the shadow said.

I was ecstatic to discover my friend had validated my selection. The warmth of the ominous presence tickled my core, and his words made me chuckle. I will credit my comrade for the prediction because the heinous man did end up as my second husband. As I finished the rest of my lukewarm tea, I smiled toward the corner.

From that moment forward, things moved swiftly. It took husband number two less than a week to ask me for my hand in marriage. I will spare you the predictable details of his proposal and courting gestures; all you must know is that he gave me many gifts, most of which were jewelry. He gave me so much jewelry I often snuck out at night and traded it to merchants in the alley for gold sovereigns to add to my nest egg. The man was so wealthy and self-absorbed that he didn't notice; in fact, he didn't bother paying attention to anything that might classify me as an actual human being. He wasn't capable of an emotional connection past surface level, which became especially clear the day after our matrimony. Quickly I learned I typically could remain unscathed if I complied with the bulk of his rules.

You should know his extermination didn't happen immediately following the ceremony. Unlike my previous marriage, If I were to stay under the radar, I had to premeditate his demise and couldn't act carelessly. To make our cohabitation more manageable, I learned to take refuge in my chamber and lock my door when the clock chimed eight. Often he arrived home between eight and nine after an afternoon and early evening of drinking at the men's club. Without fail, the mix of alcohol and testosterone-filled conversation erased his ability to hear the word "no." After trial and error, I found the best method of survival was to hide in my room during his entrance and wait until he passed out from his overconsumption of liquor. Only then would I not have to deal with him until morning.

Besides talking about himself, he loved to blather about hunting. His obsession was repulsive, and it filled his study with the carcasses of the animals he had slain. He often made people uncomfortable during dinner parties by discussing each animal's final breaths and struggle to survive. While hearing his horrific accounts, I found guzzling the table wine the best way to numb my ears. The only thing that kept me sane through our short weeks of marriage was the comforting fact he would soon be dead.

One morning I was blindsided by his abrupt attitude. He told me to pack for a weekend of fox hunting at the country estate. The cottage's scenery looked very similar to what I saw on the ride to the ceremony with husband number five. I guess some might say the correlation has made the memory particularly nostalgic. My first impression of the cottage was that it was quaint and cozy. It had a fireplace, with deer antlers hung on every wall. Candlelight chandeliers cast warm illumination in each dimly lit room, and the ambiance allowed my shadow friend's presence to thrive. During the first evening of our stay, my friend's dark, unceasing chatter intruded on my sleep and caused me to keep my eyes peeled throughout the night. Relentlessly the voice whispered in my ear when I awoke the following day and continued as I sat at the breakfast table. I felt like I was going insane, the murmuring echoes making me want to scream.

I recall that morning and every vivid detail as if it were yesterday. As husband number two passed me a silver serving dish filled with gelatinous red jam, mimicking the color and texture of coagulated blood, the dark voice grew louder in my head.

"I made plans for the two of us to go fox hunting today alone," husband number two said, lifting his eyebrows while gnawing on a piece of dried meat.

The sounds of his teeth chewing made me wince. Upon his words, my friend's voice fell silent.

Is his silence an indication that the special moment has arrived?

As I stared at him from across the table, my eyes fixated on the neanderthal nature behind each bite.

God, he's repulsive.

"Yes," I replied.

Even though I disagreed with the idea of killing defenseless animals, I knew he wouldn't give me a choice and I would have to go. At first, he seemed a bit perplexed by my response, but after a moment's pause he broke out in boisterous laughter.

"It wasn't a question, my dimwitted bride," he stated.

Silently I smiled back as my trembling hand used a butter knife to apply the raspberry jam to my bread. After I took just one bite to fill my nervous stomach, the man's fingers snapped for me to get up. As we exited the house, he grabbed a single gun off a display rack on the wall, then bellowed for me to follow him out the door. I must have worn an air of confusion because he stopped in his tracks to glare at me.

"Did you honestly think I would give you a gun? You wouldn't know how to operate a contraption like this."

His feet spun around in a circle as though he were dancing the waltz, and he pointed the rifle barrel at my head. Making a popping sound with his mouth, he pretended to shoot at me.

"Hand a woman a gun... Ha! Now that's a recipe for disaster," he said, shaking his head and laughing.

I saw the sick satisfaction in his dilated pupils. He lowered the gun to his side and continued out the door.

After he turned his back to me, I rolled my eyes. *Is he trying to provoke me?*

He was attempting to push my buttons with his condescension, and I despised him for it. Our trudge through the vast surrounding forest seemed like centuries to my feet. Furthermore, I would like to note that I am not sure where he learned to fox hunt, but he was clueless. Typically you have dogs, horses, and a sizable hunting party, with each assigned separate duties to ensure success. Husband number two had none of the above participating with him in the morbid sport. Even when our carriage driver had offered him assistance back at the cottage, he had refused and commanded him to stay behind.

The entire scenario seemed odd to me. The man merely sought to get a sadistic rise from slaughtering something in my presence. Without warning, he raised a hand to the sky and stopped walking; like an obedient wife, I followed suit. As I stood stationary, the cold wind picked up a few strands of my hair, causing them to dance in circles against my ice-cold face.

Why did he have to choose such a chilly day? He probably chose this day on purpose to watch me suffer even more.

Without question, he found enjoyment in my misery. I tried to follow his pointed gaze as it settled on a nearby burrow. Slowly he lifted the gun to his shoulder, then fired a shot next to the mound of dirt and impatiently waved for me to join him. As I made haste to stand next to him, he blindly extended the gun toward me.

"Take this woman," he demanded.

Before I could nod, he released the gun into my grip. Wasting no time, he sprinted to the hole to peer inside.

"Did you hit anything?" I asked through chattering teeth.

The answer was obvious, but I needed to keep up the appearance of naivete to conceal my knowledge. Intentionally ignoring my query, he bent over the top of the hole and reached inside. At that moment, I never could have predicted what would happen next. To this day, I feel ill just thinking about it.

"I didn't want to hit the stupid creatures. I just wanted to stun them," he said.

Intently I watched him lift his hand from the hole, gripping the scruff of a baby fox. As the animal cried in distress, my grip on the rifle tightened. Although the animal's horrific pleas for help were unbearable to stomach, I strained to suppress my dismay because I knew any bit of anguish I showed on my face would fuel him to hurt the innocent pup further. So I endeavored to appear complacent.

"How sweet, dear. You found a baby. So chivalrous of you to spare it," I said.

He turned to face me. "What do you mean?"

I stared in horror as he shifted his grip around the small animal's neck. His lips quivered with a smirk as he watched me squirm.

"You know these things kill poultry," he said. "Isn't it fascinating that something so helpless can grow into a mangy beast intent on destroying one's livelihood? If I eliminate the whole litter, I'll be doing my neighbors a favor." He said, looking back at the rest of the tiny bodies still huddling in the hole.

I felt helpless as his grasp tightened around the defenseless baby's neck. His eyes appeared crazed with thoughts of the items he could make from the fur and the stories he could share about their final breaths. The cruel show made my blood boil. Now, I will admit that what happened next is a bit of a blur, so please bear with me. A burst of wind tousled my hair and provoked my hands to clench the rifle more tightly.

"It is time," a deep voice called.

The sound of my friend's words should have comforted me, but the pup's screams engulfed my mind and shot daggers through my racing heart. My hands shook convulsively as I lost control of my emotions and raised the gun to rest on the flat of my shoulder. Through the scope, I aligned my eye with my husband, who remained distracted by the family of helpless foxes in the burrow. I fixed my stare on the tiny body dangling from his hand and his stark white knuckles wringing its neck. Hyperventilating, I tried to slow my breathing to regain focus and limit the movement of my quaking hands.

"Now!" the voice screeched.

My friend's shrieking urgency startled me and compelled me to jump. Before I could fully line up the shot, the flinch caused my hand to pull the trigger. The deafening sound of the gunshot prompted my hands to cover my ears and release the weapon to the forest floor. As I tried to stop my ears from ringing, I took a moment to comprehend what had just happened and saw my husband's body lying limp on the ground. Swiftly I picked up the gun and walked toward him to check for movement.

Our proximity had made the scene quite gruesome. Leaning closer, I saw the single bullet shattered the side of his skull, and bloody brain matter and skull fragments lay scattered on the ground surrounding him. The state of his body made it obvious he was dead.

As relief flooded my veins, I couldn't hold back my laughter. My talent surprised me. "Astonishing. I am an excellent shot," I said.

I heard faint whimpering and spotted the tiny animal shivering in a terrified ball next to my husband's corpse. So I slowly bent over and gently picked up the fox pup and nuzzled its soft body.

"Don't tremble, little one. You are safe now," I said.

After carefully placing the helpless creature with the others, I positioned the hunting rifle beside the corpse. Fortunately for me, the man's timing was quite perfect in terms of when he chose to gawk at the foxhole. The angle of his head allowed the shot's trajectory to be perfectly aligned, mimicking the precise angle of a self-inflicted wound. I searched the ground for the shell casing and placed it at a reasonable distance from the corpse. Next, I adjusted my hair and clothing to ensure my presentation would be appropriate for the situation. Then I collected a drop of sap on my fingertip from a nearby maple tree and rubbed the substance on my lower eyelid to make my eyes red and puffy. If I had to pretend to cry for this merciless dupe, I needed some help to spark the emotion.

Once everything was perfectly in place, I screamed bloody murder and collapsed to the ground. I had to keep up the hysterics for at least ten minutes before the carriage driver was scheduled to arrive. Fortunately, the scene was so perfect that he suspected no foul play and made it clear his mission was to assist me, the damsel in distress. As he helped me from the ground, the wind sincerely laughed at the dramatic spectacle. The driver helped me to the carriage, wrapped the body of husband number two in a blanket, and placed him in the cargo compartment. With a crack of the whip, we headed back to the estate to share the tragic news.

It was my most glorious performance yet.

The method of his demise surprised no one; many claimed it was bound to happen with his collection of weapons and obsession with shooting things. Because of the traumatic circumstance, I had the freedom to do whatever I chose without question. Soon after the funeral, I informed the staff that I would be going on an extended holiday to gather my thoughts, and no one queried my decision. I packed my clothing, jewelry, and cache of gold sovereigns and followed the servants as they carried my bags to the entrance. The moment I stepped out the door, much to my amazement, a carriage that looked ghostly familiar awaited me.

The image of the black carriage with a black stallion brought me warmth, and I knew I would not be returning. I watched as the old gentleman hopped from the jockey spot and loaded my luggage. Pausing a moment to say farewell, I pivoted to take one last glance at the house, and I swear I saw my second husband in the upstairs window, waving to me with that cynical smile. After stepping into the carriage, I let out a relaxing sigh and braced my hands on the seat beside me to ground myself. Letting my eyes close, I dreamt about embarking on my next adventure.

A hand shakes my leg and my eyes jolt open. "Wake up, miss. We're almost there! It would be best if you looked alive," Joseline says.

My hands rub my eyes and my mouth yawns.

I really must control my exhaustion better.

Staring out the window, I see a modest wedding chapel in the distance and pinch my cheeks to make them rosy.

Let the show begin.

Clenching my fists, I feel the shadow's grin in the corner of the carriage as we pull up to the chapel.

"*Opa*," says the shadow.

Chapter Five

HOW TALL?

T he carriage wheels come to a screeching halt. Both horses leading the way pull the taut reins and whinny as they rear up on their hindquarters. Joseline's gaze grows wide with fright, and I swear I see her witness her life flash before her eyes. Wedging her arms between the walls of the coach like a tree, she attempts to stabilize herself in the swaying compartment. It's quite the spectacle.

"Oh, my, we must have arrived," she giggles nervously.

"You don't say," I reply.

The carriage driver's lack of competency is appalling. Truth be told, his ineptitude does not surprise me. I don't expect any items of exceptional quality from husband number five, especially after he willingly purchased the gaudy dress on my body and thought the material to be acceptable for the ceremony. He's lucky I'm not fussy; any other woman would have thrown a fit. In all actuality, I selected the man to take the sought-after seat of husband number five due to his fraudulent behavior. His personality thrives off his living a lavish lifestyle without having the means to financially back his persona.

To disguise his secret, he utilizes something I refer to as the white knight syndrome. What is this syndrome, you ask? Since it is my wedding day, you have found me in an excellent mood, and I will happily be your educator. The term depicts someone who has a savior complex. Some individuals purchase gifts, such as flowers, in order to buy affection. They use flashy items and their wealth to court, almost like investing in expensive fishing lures made of gold. White knight syndrome presents courting strategies that can, on the surface, appear similar to what one would expect, but the underlying intent is markedly different. Men who use this scheme are considerably more conniving than run-of-the-mill suitors.

They favor using extreme tactics of manipulation to get what they want. Unbeknownst to you, they create scenarios that place you in the position of the damsel in distress. By crafting problematic situations that are difficult to solve alone, they, in a sense, demoralize you. White knights exploit your vulnerability, taking control of your emotional state by swooping in to save you from the distressing circumstance orchestrated at their hands. Think about it. Wouldn't you fall for the hero who saved you from a jarring situation? In children's tales, doesn't the knight win the princess after slaying a fire-breathing dragon? Abundantly aware we have been groomed since childhood to fall for cordial gentlemen, these men prey on our naivete for romance. Rescuing a victim from a trauma-induced psychological response assures a battered underdog's dependency. The predator wants to be the only one you trust, and through this calculating tactic, he can accomplish just that.

You may wonder if you can identify someone's intentions from their outer appearance. Shame on you; I shall slap your wrists for thinking such preposterous thoughts! You merely feed into a ploy that allows them to get away with their horrible behavior because of how we interpret their shell.

Didn't the parental figure in your life ever tell you not to judge a book by its cover? Society's cookie-cutter narrative usually describes the grand hero as attractive—which is utter horse shit.

On that note, let us ask ourselves what the word "attractive" means. Isn't the phrase objective for both you and me? I believe men made up the term to cause others to anguish over their born attributes. The word is quite degrading and infuriating. I am not a betting woman, but if asked to vouch for my opinion by throwing all my money on a card table, I would happily do so. It is sad to think I am the only one willing to be honest with you. Someone should be judged by their intellectual contributions to society and the mark they leave behind, not by how fuckable their peers deem them. I mean, bloody hell, we all might as well work in the sex industry if that's our only contribution of value. Life could be one massive orgy for which no female contributors receive payment. If push comes to shove, the occasional sale of one's privates wouldn't be so treacherous to keep the books stacked, would it? The only downside to the plan would be the horrible market saturation; the competition would be unbearable. Honestly, my hypothesis sends a shuddering sensation through my bones.

Before I get carried away addressing the more significant issues regarding our societal stereotypes, I will resume our original discussion regarding the white knight syndrome.

Since we're in an honest relationship, feel free to stop me if you sense I'm starting to go on yet another tangent.

Let us recommence, my cherished acquaintances. In most fairy tales, the knight character whom the princess marries is habitually depicted as svelte and chiseled. His jawline is often compared to that of a Greek God and his torso to a washboard. His form is statuesque, and he possesses an ideal physique. The author's description of the man makes the reader believe he can swoon a woman by looks alone, with or without being the hero figure. Since he is blatantly attractive, it is a win for the woman, regardless of his heroic feat. The notion of him chivalrously saving her is just a bonus for the storyline and placed to fuel our unrealistic relationship expectations.

Now prepare your eyes for some discouraging news. The knight prototype women have been raised to seek doesn't exist, and if you happen to encounter the overzealous goings-on I mentioned in my preceding white night lecture, run or be wary at the least. Together we must decry the false ideas force-fed to our innocent minds and rally to burn the stereotypes to which we are shackled.

Because I believe there can never be enough lighthearted laughter, I will give you a comical comparison you might enjoy. Now that I have your attention, I will disclose the identity of all white knight syndrome perpetrators; the answer is quite simple: they are smelly wart-laden bridge trolls. If only that were true, it would make identifying the perpetrators so much simpler.

In all seriousness, the outer package of the nonfictional white knight is generally very unexpected and typically comes across as safe or nonthreatening. Often the heroic deeds these individuals perform are only used to divert attention from their shortcomings, which can mean countless things. Dependent on the person's insecurities, they may try to mask their shortcomings in areas such as outward form, stature, behavior, or disposition.

Unfortunately, the white knight syndrome doesn't end with concocted rescue scenarios. After ensnaring your trust with their faux nobility, they kindle your empathy by sharing stories of the oppression they have faced. They may reveal they are a walking target for societal jokes. A typical talking point may be the many ways life has cheated them out of their happiness. Their mind refuses to let go of the toxic memories they blame for their internal misery, and they believe it is your responsibility to bear their burdens. They take great pleasure in revenge, believing they are owed your charitable compliance, and God help you if you don't appease their demands. They are most dangerous.

Occasionally the actions they use as fodder are easily recognizable. For example, they may choose to spread a negative rumor involving your character around town. As everyone questions your identity, you may lose faith in yourself and join the masses, pondering where the truth lies. The gossip could be something fundamental, such as "I heard her pearls are fake." You should know they are not picky with the pettiness fueling the comment. All they are focused on is how you will react to the gossip. The topic they choose to feed to the piranha pool is something they already know makes you feel self-conscious.

Perceived as doting listeners, white knights are notorious for gathering mental lists containing sensitive topics they discover in their intimate conversations with you. Trust me;

they do not wish to ruin you, only knock you down a few pegs. Once you become flustered by the judgment of your peers, they will begin their descent to save you from your poor self-esteem by championing an effort to build back your confidence. Behind closed doors, they may say things like, "I don't know who would ever say something so vile" or "Don't worry; I know you're an outstanding person, and I'll do everything I can to set the narrative straight."

You see, they want to make it known they are the reason the torment stops. In the victimizer's sick mind, the powerful gesture forces you to be emotionally indebted to them, and they'll never let you forget it. You can never escape their hold after they rescue you from the situation in which they played the role of grand puppet master. The grim reality of the toxic circumstance is they, not society, are the bullies and the sole reason for your fluctuating self-esteem. They want you to believe everyone is plotting against you and they're the only ones willing to fight for your integrity.

Manipulation isn't the only way this toxic tendency exhibits itself; it also rears its ugly head in monetary schemes. Let me use the universally understood example of giving and receiving gifts from a significant other. Imagine if someone bought you a gift. I know that thought brings you happiness, as it does to most. What if the giver purchased something they expected you'd find unsatisfying? Since the point of giving a gift is usually to make someone happy, their motive may naturally confuse you. You may wonder why they chose something they knew would trigger the opposite response one would hope for. It is simply part of the bigger plan to keep you mentally trapped. If you constantly question the reality in which you live, they know you will never have the strength to leave.

Upon seeing your disappointment in the present, they will offer an outlandish explanation regarding how the selection of the substandard item wasn't their fault, followed by disdaining words that detail their great sacrifice and your ungrateful depletion of their finances. Upon completing their rant, they will ensure that you second-guess your reaction and every word that departed your lips. The timing of the next phase will vary as they wait for your apology before proceeding. When you appear defeated, they will surprise you with another gift to replace the first one, and the selection will be a slight step above the last. Regardless of your true feelings, you will think it marvelous because the perpetrator has conditioned you regarding how to feel. They are already embedded in your head.

He performs this clownish act to hide the fact he can never afford the top-end gift he knows you deserve. Rather than owning up to his actual financial status, he prefers to tear down your opinions and eliminate the possibility that you'll ever question him. As a result of his manipulation, you willingly accept the second mediocre gift. He feels victorious after meeting his objective and can continue his facade without question. It is all a ploy of control and a grooming tactic to make you believe he's the only one who cares. The monster is trying to isolate you.

Joseline acts more excited than I do about my ceremony as she peers out the window at the lush scenery. "Come look, miss! It is your husband-to-be that stopped our ride," she says.

Oh, God.

"Hurry. You must see this. He's carrying a grand bouquet! It's oh-so-romantic!"

Reluctantly I force a smile and scoot myself toward the window to take a gander. Seeing me approach, Joseline moves out of the way. Although the spectacle outside the carriage is absurd, the sight is not disappointing. It lives up to the maid's brief description and then some; he's even more ridiculous than I expected. Though our carriage is already stock-still, he continues to wave his hands to stop it. One horse furrows its nose in the air as it recoils, trying to protect its head from the man's ridiculously flailing limbs. The highlight is seeing the flowers fall from his hand to the ground. Quickly he leans over to frantically pick them up.

I don't think he realizes I'm watching him. After gathering the flowers at his feet, he stands upright and brushes the dirt off each rosebud. As he shifts the flowers to his side, I finally catch a glimpse of his outfit and am immediately aware of his true fashion sense. His ridiculous clothing choice exudes the aura of an individual faking wealth. Initially I thought his selection of my tacky gown was accidental, but apparently, it's the man's characteristic style. In between his dress shirt pleats sit layers upon layers of ivory ruffles, which his sleeves perfectly match. Around his neck, he dons an enormously large collar that lies open on each side of his chest. Due to his intentional unbuttoning, the low-cut opening exposes patchy clusters of hair that mimic an unhealthy lawn. The shirt looks as though it was selected from a pirate ship's closet. Enough about the shirt's details; I find one particular attribute of his highly distracting: he's so short that he barely reaches the necks of the noble steeds that pull his carriage. The sight confuses me, as I cannot decipher if the horses are extra large or if he's extra small. Since I might seem taken aback by his characteristics, there is something I must explain.

You see, the way I met him was quite different, and this experience is something new to me. Unlike my other suitors, whom I met through in-person encounters, our courting occurred exclusively through letter writing. I committed to the man sight unseen. The entire experience is quite baffling due to the untraditional nature of our courtship, and I'm confident your interest regarding the details of our introduction has been piqued, so let me explain the situation at hand. While still shackled to husband number four, I began a pen pal journey with husband number five. During my previous marriage, I had devised ways to make my future transitions with each new suitor smoother, and I found myself confounded by my swirling thoughts. Then, on one exceptionally ordinary day, everything changed. As I picked up the morning paper from our stoop, I was met with an interesting sight.

Usually, I found the paper perfectly rolled and left on the step for me to fetch, but the presentation was different this time. When I retrieved the newspaper, it was unrolled and had been left open to a particular page, exposing a sizable black ink smear that encircled a paragraph. Being the voracious reader I am, I was thrilled to find a new section added to my morning delivery. As I took a closer look, I had to chuckle and give thanks to my friend, who hid in the shadows of a nearby alley. The new section detailed eligible bachelors from across the country, all interested in finding a companion. Underneath each name was an address for correspondence. Before placing the paper on the breakfast table for my fourth husband to peruse, I used a pencil and paper to trace the article's contents. After stashing it away for later, I patiently waited until dusk to read the contents and found the nobleman who currently raises his hands like Moses in front of the horses.

When I initially wrote to the peculiar man, we never discussed physical characteristics such as height. I had based my mental image of his appearance on the newspaper's cunning illustration of him, which offered a vague likeness of his general shape. Upon seeing him in the flesh, I discern each slightly over-embellished detail, and I am being generous with my use of the word "slightly."

Beggars can't be choosers, I think, trying to shift my mindset away from ridiculing him.

Following suit with the article's misrepresentation of his outward appearance, his statements were equally preposterous. In fact, they were one of the main reasons I pursued him. Although the fallacies regarding his physical appearance initially eluded me, my nose could easily sniff out the fictitious details when reading his overselling list of devilish accomplishments. For example, he listed "prize-holding lover" as an attribute. His insane choice of words told me he was either hiding a secret or, realistically, was a compulsive liar. To be fair, both options equate to terrible personality traits. Either way, I decided he was the perfect candidate for my subsequent marriage.

Upon discovering his flawed character, I wasted no time sending the first letter with the primary motive of luring him into marriage. I was confident that if I could get him to propose, it would take him off the market, and the horrible article would be forsaken and burned.

He could no longer use his fibbing tales to con another woman. His predictability validated that I was where I was supposed to be, and from then on, I found everything working out exactly as I'd expected. When our confidential communication escalated, it was time for husband number four to croak. It was by far my smoothest transition yet.

Abrupt tiny knocks on the carriage door pull me back to the present. Glaring out the window, I catch a glimpse of a small man's balding head positioned in front of the backdrop of the chapel—his hairpiece flaps in the breeze like a one-winged albatross attempting to fly in a windstorm.

"You can't let him see you peering through the window, miss!" Joseline admonishes me.

Oh, right, this is my husband-to-be.

I keep forgetting his authentic appearance. For some reason, I visualized the enormity of his obnoxious personality to match his size, not try to compensate for it. Also, I've never seen the chambermaid have as much ambition as she does now. Lunging across the cabin, she uses her body to block me from the window. I'm stunned as I'm knocked back to my seat and watch her open the door. Honestly, if she wants to talk to my almost-husband, she is free to do so; no spectacle is needed. I have no issue with prolonging our first face-to-face conversation.

"You cannot see the bride before the wedding, Sir Fitz. It is bad luck," she says through the slight crack in the door.

"Very well then. Will you please at least give her the flowers I purchased?" he asks.

Petals fly everywhere as his tiny hand wedges the bouquet through the small opening. I cannot understand why he is so persistent with forcing them through the microscopic crack; they are a minor expense. He is more concerned with establishing control over the situation than protecting the bouquet. If the man wished to respect others' boundaries, he would have asked before thrusting the shrubbery inside. The shrubs do not even make it fully into the coaches' interior before half the buds are on the floor.

"Of course. That is quite fine, sir," Joseline says, accepting the gift.

As she shuts the door, he speaks again. "Wait! Be sure to send her my apologies for the poor floral selection. Tell her I shall fire the gardener when we return home. It was his fault it is not as grand as promised."

I'm relieved by the sound of the door shutting in his face, as each word made my eyes roll. Why is he lying? Shouldn't he be more concerned about whether I am allergic or have an affection for flowers? I already know it wasn't the gardener's fault. Now all I can think of is some poor gardener losing his job because this fool wishes to cover up his defects. Don't you remember our discussing this? He just hit the tip of the iceberg for performing as the white knight. Mark my words: he will prove the verdict by evening's end, and you will laugh with me. Prepare your champagne flutes because you will owe me a toast.

We annoyingly wait for a solid half-hour in the musty carriage for him to leave. His bullheadedness is even more unattractive than his physical appearance. As soon as Joseline sees his partially glued floating toupee is clear from her sightline, she calls me toward the exit. Stepping outside to get fresh air has never made me feel better; the man's obnoxious personality was severely testing my patience.

Once outside and able to breathe, I find the open space sheds light on the suffocating nature of his attempt at passive control. The brief encounter with him made it quite apparent the reason behind the maid's anxious nature and justified a number of her behaviors. It was infuriating to me. Hypothetically he would get complete control over me after our marriage, so his current impatience seemed unjustified. The fact that he wouldn't allow me a second to calm my thoughts disheartened me, and it was apparent he would stop at nothing if it meant momentarily relinquishing his control.

I take a deep breath as I hear the organ begin to play inside the chapel. Each note echoes, reminding me of the short walk I have ahead of me. Beyond any doubt, I know what his tactic is. It's apparent he instructed them to play so I'll move faster. My trek across the grassy field feels like a lifetime as hatred fuels each of my steps. I pay no attention as Joseline picks up the train from my gown so it remains white. All the while, my thoughts continue to spiral.

If a game is what he wants, I shall give him one he surely will never forget, I think with a chuckle.

Joseline turns around to watch me laugh and smiles. "That's the spirit! You should be giddy on your wedding day!"

If the child knew the thoughts racing through my mind, she would tone down her enthusiasm.

"Indeed!" I reply.

Not knowing how to respond to my overexuberance, she falls silent for the rest of the walk. As we finish our venture toward the chapel's front doors, the reality of the situation sets in. Although I want to run, I still have a critical mission to accomplish.

Joseline swats at my hand as I reach for the chapel door to let myself inside. "Not yet, miss. You must wait for your cue."

Her finger points to the sky like a conducting stick waving to the beat of the music. As the brash organ does a slow climb up an off-key scale, a high note plays, and the pitch falls sharp. The sound makes me wince.

"Now!" she says.

My eyes widen as Joseline dramatically places her hands on the door handles.

That must be my cue. I smirk. *Let the performance begin.*

Chapter Six

OLD HORSE NEW TRICKS

As the doors open, I feel transported to another dimension. Although I acknowledge the decorative achievements my betrothed has thrust upon the world should wow me, I sense nothing of the sort. Rather than appearing extraordinary, the artistic choices are quite ordinary indeed, and the decorations had every sign of being salvaged. To be honest, I would not be shocked if they were still hanging from a ceremony the week before. Crinkled white satin ribbons drape across each pew, accented with hanging bells made from faded tissue paper. Rose petals scatter the ground beneath me. A depressed individual petal lays at my foot, catching my attention.

I notice every discolored hole as I inspect the lonely petal, and the sick metaphor makes me laugh. I'm positive my murky friend must have planted the sad statement as an omen for my betrothed's dwindling life. Having been through this ceremony more times than most, I acknowledge I can be a harsher critic than the typical bride. If I were to compare this occasion to all my previous weddings,

I would still find the setup severely disappointing. Should I be surprised he hasn't my expectations? The reality of the situation is simple: he has never lived up to any of his tales, big or small. Believe me, the pun was intended, and my metaphor does not exclude his height.

An eggplant-colored argyle carpet lines the walkway between the pews. As my eyes skip to each stain, they lead me to glare at grand Fitz standing at the altar. The sound of the wooden double doors shutting behind me triggers his body to move. Slowly he swivels to gawp in my direction and gives an exaggerated glance of surprise, pretending my presence has thrown him off guard. The dramatic expression induces his eyes to become broad and his forehead to crease. All in all, I find the spectacle ridiculous. When he cued the orchestra to start early, he knew full well it would force me to the chapel.

Let me explain the term "orchestra" so my words don't lead you astray. Typically this word is used to describe a group of performers, but in this case, the ensemble is composed of a single organist. I dare say his dilated pupils look just as thrilled as mine. With each pounding stroke of every sticky key, his eyes drift into a daydream. Since he's the only musician here, one might think he would be extra cautious to stay tuned, but the abrasive music tells the captive audience another story. Each plunked note causes his excitement to heighten and the large powdered white wig sitting on top of his shiny skull to teeter. The scene reminds me of an outlandish carnival. Just as I think the over-ratted top piece might finally escape, he raises a hand to the sky and slaps the tousled wig back into place. The question of which creature's wiry hair was used to craft such a specimen makes my eyes squint with curiosity.

My wandering mind returns to reality as the organist's clunky hands aggressively hit the keys to play the final chord of the hymn. The brash cluster of sounds makes my body wince and fists tighten. In an attempt to redirect my harsh criticism, my mind replays an aria from an operatic performance I once enjoyed. The unexpected sound of Fitz's loud applause quickly pulls me from my reminiscence, though, and gives me hope the musical number has ended. A deep breath escapes my chest, revealing my confusion.

Is it done?

Watching my husband-to-be jump up and down like a schoolboy does not cross me as unpredictable. What is off-putting, however, is the moment his small finger points to the musician. The action incites my already-dwindling respect to plummet drastically. Initially I can't decipher what he's trying to accomplish with the flailing metatarsal. His obscene rally for others to join his colorful celebration, however, allows me to quickly deduce the motive of his actions. He is oddly proud of the spectacle and wants others to feel the same. Every clap of his hands is a sad attempt to initiate resounding applause for the artist. To compensate for the lack of camaraderie, he loudly kisses each finger in the direction of the wigged man.

"Isn't he just mesmerizing?" Husband number five announces, his hands frantically circling in the air.

Diverting my honest response, I clear my throat and prevent my eyes from rolling. Just as my focus loosens, Joseline's hands vigorously join in the applause. The building sound causes the musician's head to jolt up to the sky as if it awoke him from a long nap. He appears to have forgotten where he is or suddenly detected the repercussions of overdrinking. Either way, his spatial awareness is no longer with us. Just as I think he's taking his final bow to address his two fans, his fingers surprise the masses and launch into the traditional bridal processional. The sight of my soon-to-be husband waiting for me at the altar causes a stabbing sensation to ascend in my gut. I force an uncomfortable smile across my lips to compensate for the striking pain.

"Indeed," I answer.

The small agreeance felt impossible to release. If the man's blind taste for frivolous things weren't enough to detour any reasonable woman from matrimony, his tone-deaf ears surely would be. As Joseline gleefully moves down the aisle, my lower limbs refuse to budge. She makes it a quarter of the way down the matrimonial pathway before turning back to notice my stagnant body. Redirecting her course, she rushes toward me to lend a hand.

"We all get a little nervous sometimes," she says quietly, then tugs my arm.

My feet refuse every one of her nudging attempts, taking hold like roots into the ground. As she gives one last pull on my arm, her lips purse to let out a soft grunt. The momentum drives my feet to move down the stained carpet while the music plays louder. Zeroing my gaze on the end of the aisle, I lock eyes with my fiancé and coyly smile. Unable to read my thoughts, he takes my facial expression as an ogle of enchanted bliss. As I continued forward, the sound of a nearby wooden pew creaking piques my interest, and my glance shifts to look at the perpetrator creating the ruckus.

What I am about to disclose provokes my stomach to drop and reeks of surprise. My bevy of deceased husbands sits in a line halfway down the hellish row of benches. They're the reason behind each creak plaguing my subconscious. At first, I thought my mind was playing tricks on me, but as my feet carried me closer, I realized their apparitions were real. One by one, their corpses wait for my body to pass the pew. As I approach, I watch with terror as each of the men's heads turns and gawks at my frame. In my mind, I froze all four of their appearances in time, allowing me to reflect on my last visual memories of them. The gory sight sends my mind tumbling on trails of cartwheels as I attempt to communicate with them through telepathy and prissy facial expressions.

If you're trying to haunt me, your attempt is more depressing than your pointless lives.

Slowing my pace walk, I inconspicuously endeavor to get a better look. I glimpse my first husband stationed farthest from the aisle, glaring at me with his hatred-filled coal-black eyes. Well, what's left of them anyway. To be frank, I forgot how badly each book's whack bludgeoned his skull. The craters look like a Grand Canyon of sorts, and the blunt trauma to the top of his head compacted his eye sockets and made his eyes putrid. His blue lips slowly grin, revealing bits of paper from my cherished atlas wedged between his teeth.

Gargantuanly stationed next to him, waiting for his turn to garner my attention, is husband number two. Their head injuries complement each other surprisingly well, making them look like brothers. Half of his skull is cleanly missing, and his face droops with a rude sneer. From his expression, I take it he is not enthused that the extended barrel of his gun caused his death. His hacked, hanging jaw causes drool to fall onto his lapel and his throat to make gurgling noises. Any annunciation of words is absent due to the bullet having severed the small muscle beneath his tongue. Knowing he can no longer make complete sentences brings me great relief. I'm sure his comrades appreciate his lack of speech, or they would if they were privy to his true personality. If they weren't aware of how much he loves to boast about himself, it would be hard for them to understand how lucky they are to meet him now, in his grotesque inarticulate condition.

Honestly, I'm tickled he isn't capable of smiling. With his treacherous behavior toward animals, he should never be granted any small moments of satisfaction that might result in a grin. As my eyes move down the line of corpses, I can see the identity of the next member of the boys' club plain as day. The image of my third husband's wrinkled appearance rushes through my mental cavity.

Oh, Jesus, the crypt keeper.

Deep in my core, I feel elements of surprise. One would never imagine crotchety old number three would be vigorous enough to make the occasion. I'm not embarrassed or concerned by his withered looks; it is the old man's devil-worshiping character I loathe. Please do not interpret my words literally; he is not a true Satanist. When he was alive, he would attend the local church on holidays with his offspring from his previous betrothals. I'm sure my description has summoned your interest; naturally you're wondering about the dear fellow's identity and the story of how we met. This is the longest wedding processional I have ever experienced; you'll be excited to learn we have time to kill. My feet shall slow their pace down the rest of the walkway so I may share my story regarding husband number three. Please do not concern yourself about husband number five's reaction to my slow arrival. In all fairness, he will attribute my sloth-like walk to my serene dreaminess over marrying him.

When we last chatted about my past marriages, dear readers, we were delving into the aftermath of my time with husband number two. If I correctly recall, I had just leaped into the black carriage to make my departure from his estate, and unlike the times before, I was able to take a trunk of necessities with me. As I watched the prime estate leave my line of sight, I became hopeful about what the future would hold, as I was now free to leave the town and pleased to relinquish any aforementioned stress. Even though I expected to change my name with my new beginning, I found the security I yearned for quenched by pocketing an identity I could fall back on. The assurance of having a place to return to made me feel invincible.

Like the last time, I let the shadow direct the carriage's trajectory for my landing. With my friend keeping me safe thus far, I had every reason to put all faith into the mysterious being. About six hours into the long ride, my eyes closed, and I drifted off into a dreaming state of blissfulness. If asked, I couldn't honestly tell you how long I stayed in that peaceful slumber, but when my eyes opened, I found myself in the town of Ashfalls. Although it was a peculiar name for a village, the ambiance was quaint and appealing.

Amid a damp fog, the sound of a cracking whip in the town square signaled my arrival. Looking out the window, I saw the exterior of a plush Inn. It didn't just look like any Inn; it was unique and exuded prestige that caught my intrigue. A vacancy sign rested on the ornate wooden entry door to lure me inside. The exterior walls were constructed of beautiful dark stone and fruitful grapevines strategically wrapped across the mortar lines. After noticing my belongings had been offloaded outside, I opened the door, let myself out of the passenger compartment, and walked to fetch my chest. Confusion rushed over me as I turned back toward the carriage to pay, and the man was nowhere to be found.

I spun in circles, searching for the gentleman who had delivered me to my new home, but again I found no sign of him or the carriage. The entire account was particularly odd to me. Before I had used this driver, I'd never met someone so frivolous with collecting payment for their service. The fact that he was agreeable to leaving a woman like me alone in the street was unnerving. Despite his having offloaded my bags without charging me, I would think he'd check for my safety. Anyway, enough with him; I will continue with the story at hand.

As I stood outside the prestigious inn with my heavy trunk, I must have appeared helpless to onlookers because it was only a moment before someone rushed to my aid. A bell jingled as the inn's front door swung open. I turned to see who had opened the door and was greeted by an older man. He wore an elaborate suit woven with velvet piping, and he donned a beaver-felt top hat. Everything on his body was perfectly tailored and pristinely matched, displaying his affluence. Ironically, as he stood in front of the inn, the pattern of his suit camouflaged him due to the building's color-coordinated facade. Before he spoke a single word, he clapped his hands to the sky as if performing the tango; a moment later, two men dressed in red coattails promptly answered his call.

With an amiable smile, he pointed for them to fetch my heavy chest and bring it inside. I gave a nod of thanks and followed closely behind my belongings. After the men crossed the threshold, the mysterious man continued to hold the door so I could enter. As I passed through the entrance, the forced close proximity allowed me to analyze his face. Though each wrinkle accented his appearance like grooves on a tree stump, he still wasn't hard on the eyes. Due to his perfectly quaffed appearance, one might indeed call him a silver fox. The man must have been pushing seventy years of age, but he still carried his tall, lean frame like he was thirty.

As I passed through the doorway, he smiled, and his mouth opened to speak. "Welcome to my humble abode," he said with rolled diction.

The confidence he exuded from his pores was absurd. Since his looks had slightly left with age, one would assume he must have wealth to back his self-esteem. Remaining quiet, I smirked while walking past him, and the chase ensued. The interior's decoration style rivaled the excellent presentation I witnessed outside. Every detail was impressionable, and I could tell a keen eye had selected it. When my eyes fixated on the ornate wooden front counter across from the marbled entry, I made my way to check in for a room. As I made haste toward the reception desk, I detected the sound of the older gentleman's heeled boots echoing behind me. Ignoring his eager perseverance, I quickened my pace and swayed my hips.

Finally I reached the counter, where the bellman quickly gathered my luggage. His behavior perturbed me, and I cleared my throat with a high pitch to show my disapproval. As I patiently waited for assistance, I realized the reason for the bellman's shifting demeanor was due to the elderly gentleman's fast-approaching presence. When he reached the counter, he motioned for the bellman to move aside to make room for him, then pretended to know how to perform the day-to-day job of receptionist. He daintily lifted a spectacle to his left eye while scanning the reservation list, striving to look uninterested while he thumbed through the pages.

"Are you traveling alone?" he asked.

"Yes, I am indeed alone," I said, trying to read the guest list.

The sound of voice made him look up from the list of names. His lips quivered with a slight grin, and he removed his spectacle to get a better look at my face. His mannerisms became giddy, like those of a gleeful schoolboy.

"How modern of you to travel, alone," he said.

I responded with a forged giggle to mask my true feelings over the insolent query. Despite wanting to vomit, I found something about the man alluring, which fueled my desire to learn more about him. As he searched for his next topic of conversation, he blatantly admired my cleavage.

"I take it you fancy reading too," he said.

How would he know what I like?

I could tell the man was well traveled and wiser than others I had encountered. To bide time, I took a moment to softly clear my throat while searching for an appropriate reply to his assertion.

"Perhaps," I said.

He refocused his line of sight to idolize my corseted waist and contradicted his feigned harmless curiosity by moistening his lips with his tongue. "If you choose to stay, our establishment has an entire library for your enjoyment."

Waiting for my response, he locked gazes with me.

Feeding into the suspense, I took my time and pursed my lips before replying. "Is that so?" I asked.

My words seemed to excite the man, making his feet fervently tap the floor. Paying attention to his mannerisms, I noticed the timbre of his voice heighten in pitch.

"Oh, you bet your bottom we do! We have every relevant novelist and poet right at your fingertips."

"Oh, my, I dare say I would be foolish not to take a room," I said.

Before he uttered another word, I reached into my cleavage and pulled out a mass of folded pound notes. I was shocked his heart didn't give out at the sight of my fingers going between my pushed-up breasts. As he eyed the money in my hand, his face relaxed and he grinned. The pitch of my voice softened as I used the cash to fan my face with fresh air.

"Pardon my lack of manners," I said. "I forgot to ask to whom I have the pleasure of speaking."

My shift to a sultry tone prompted the older man to gulp and loosen the fashionable scarf around his neck. "Why, I am Harold, the owner of this fine establishment," he said, grandly motioning to the surroundings.

Pretending to look impressed, I forced eye contact with the fellow.

He leaned over the counter to get closer to me. "I must know the name of the gorgeous lady who has stopped my heart."

Although his words made me shudder, I maintained my composure. "Francis," I told him.

"Such an enchanting name. I would love to hear your thoughts on literature sometime, my dear guest."

Even though he emanated a predatory aura, I politely nodded. I wanted to decipher his personality sufficiently, I needed to get to know the fellow.

"Yes, that would be lovely," I said.

"Over a cup of tea, perhaps?"

An afternoon meeting seemed harmless, so I agreed to his solicitation.

"Indeed," I said through gritted teeth.

The smile he gave to my reply still haunts me to this day. It felt as if he had me exactly where he wanted me, like a mouse trapped by a single leg in a sprung trap. Before his outstretched hand could feel the temperature of my skin, I quickly grabbed the keys from his palm and made haste to my room. The red-uniformed men placed the trunk in my quarters and left me alone for the evening. I must say, for what it's worth, this man's inn was pristinely built and provided excellent service.

Waking up the following day felt glorious. As I rolled over in bed, I wasn't tasked with having to look at another being. If someone tells you staring at another soul upon waking is the highlight of their day, they're lying to you. We, as creatures, do better with independence, and their words are just a ploy to make you feel guilty about leaving. Because of his age, I didn't want to put the target of husband number three upon his back until I had concrete proof of his ill intentions.

While I prepared to have tea with the fellow, I wore nothing seductive, allowing my judgment of him to be based solely on his unprovoked behavior. The last thing I wanted was to provide bait for the fellow. All the analyses I was about to make needed to be organically perceived.

Upon entering the tearoom for our meeting, I tried to clear my mind of any preconceived notions. Like any gentleman who seems harmless, he pulled out my chair and poured my brew. Considering his kind actions, I thought I had drastically misjudged the man. Oh, dear, had my initial judgment been proved wrong?

As I blew on the hot cup to cool the steeping liquid, I opened my mouth to discuss my favorite works of literature.

"What do you like to read?" I asked.

"What?" he replied.

Knowing good and well he had heard what I'd asked, I gave a moment of silence. I hoped he would restructure his response and answer my inquisition within the allotted time. Instead of taking the hint, however, he excitedly changed the subject.

"I know a topic we will both find exhilarating!" he said.

"Do tell..."

He leaned forward. "How many men have you had between the sheets?"

The disrespectful question made me choke on my tea.

"Excuse me?" I replied.

By leaning closer to me, he made it abundantly clear he saw nothing inappropriate about the question. Rather than change the direction of the conversation, he determined the only issue with his inquiry was his presentation, so he lowered his voice and spoke more slowly.

"You're an attractive woman, so I'm sure you've had your fair share of fun," he said.

To deescalate the situation and reroute our topic, I answered in a way he would not find prudish or enticing. "I must admit I'm a secretive woman when it comes to my romantic life," I said, calming my quaking hands.

"Oh, my, I see what is happening. You surely didn't think I was only interested in discussing novels. I mean, look at you, Francis... Your body is superb," he said, gawking at me.

My hand clenched around the handle of the ornately painted teacup. Yet another man who didn't value a woman for her intellect. Even though his behavior disappointed me, I had to look unfazed. A fake smile stained my face to cover my uncomfortable feelings.

"Of course not. That would be silly of me," I said.

"From the moment I laid eyes on you when you were traveling alone, I knew you differed from the rest of them. Finding a financially stable woman who isn't a prude is like finding a needle in a haystack."

I nodded. "I understand."

During the rest of our conversation over tea, he asked a vast number of inappropriate questions. Since the queries and responses were one-sided, you'd think the man would have gotten the hint that I had no interest in the topics, but the old pervert continued. With each new question I wished to forget, I reluctantly entertained him to get through our chitchat. When I took the final sip of my cup, he asked if he could make a physical advance, and I allowed him a stray kiss on the back of my hand. I cringed at every word that followed the act and couldn't imagine my lips kissing the fellow.

From our encounter, he undoubtedly deduced we were compatible. After I returned to my room, he paid for my stay, and he requested my hand in marriage within a week. It was a whirlwind, to say the least, and by the end, I'd never felt more disgusted. Each night I took two baths to rid my skin of the sickening feeling his touch induced. The only thing that kept me sane through our time together was knowing he soon would no longer be predatory toward another female.

In the weeks that led up to the wedding, I moved into a guest room in his large estate, and upon my first walk around the grounds, I beheld a familiar plant in his garden. Although I immediately recognized the flower, I pretended to be naïve and asked him what it was. He told me it was just a weed, but I already had determined it was a cluster of wild poppies in early bloom.

If I were to survive the night of our nuptials without being molested, he would need to be heavily sedated, so I concocted a brilliant plan. The evening before the ceremony, I picked a dozen poppies from the garden bed, harvested the tiny black seeds, and placed as many as I could inside the locket. When we returned home from the ceremony, all my fears became a reality. The man violently forced himself upon me, which caused my shadow friend to grow in the room's corner with rage.

I will spare you most of the disturbing details to protect your unsullied mind—and honestly, I wish not to relive it. To this day, the mere thought of the wind from his breath against my neck makes my skin crawl and body shudder. Rest assured, I shoved the contents of my locket into his mouth and forced him to swallow every seed. I wrapped the necklace in a silken handkerchief and hid it in the bottom of my trunk. Upon his unconscious convulsions, I called for a doctor and unleashed my hysterics like a seasoned thespian. In death, I can thank my husband for adding to the realism of my traumatized emotions by his rape of me. I believe it might have helped sell my alibi. When the doctor arrived, he did not give my involvement in the man's demise a second thought.

As it was our marital night and he was partially nude, the doctor attributed my husband's death to old age. He ruled his heart had naturally given out from the excitement. As the undertaker left with the body, I sat alone in the dark bedroom, comforted only by my shadowed friend throughout the night.

"The horrible creature is gone," it kept repeating.

The memory of my previous actions that night thrust my thoughts into a dark entrancing state. The shadow was right and, as always, looked out for me. To help me overcome my traumatic experience, my next suitor was almost instantly awarded to me. As his insatiable brood was concerned I would spend their inheritance; his son immediately offered his hand in marriage to exude his control and have eyes on the situation. Trust me when I say the apple doesn't fall far from the tree. Considering I didn't have to make up a new identity to lure my fourth marriage, the process was relatively seamless.

The sound of the organist playing the final chord of my procession snaps me back to reality. It's my wedding day; worry over my prior husbands revealing my secrets to my new groom incites my heart to race. To calm the loud beating, I turn toward the lineup of deceased husbands, but they're gone.

Everything is grand.

Looking at the end of the marital path, I see my husband-to-be. Slightly past his head sits the shadow in the corner. I smirk.

"Oh, happy day," the voice says.

"Oh, happy day," I say with a smile.

Fitz looks at me from the altar with admiration. "Oh, happy day," he says as I approach.

We are all happy for various reasons, and I am thankful.

Chapter Seven

SEEING DOUBLE

My stomach drowns in unease as I stand at the end of the pews. Joseline hurries to the front row and sits behind me to watch the ceremony. She hunches the top half of her body over her knees and clenches her fists to control her excitement. As I look back at her, she waves to me with an open-mouthed smile, her body language contradicting my racing nerves. Honestly, I would be less agitated too if our roles were reversed.

In contrast, I'm stuck up here like a sideshow spectacle while she sits idly by, observing the grand wedding charade. If offered the same luxury, I might have a comparable attitude. Instead my eyes are dry from each bit of air slipping through the drafty stained-glass window seals and penetrating my tear ducts. Could the man have picked a less suitable venue? If I were to challenge him, the fool probably would provide something worse to prove a point.

I pivot my body to face him and look him squarely in the eye. Finally the childish man's clownish features are fully revealed, and I swear his appearance is the most off-putting of all my husbands. His eyes sit somewhat proportional on his face, but the color is problematic. The brown doesn't lighten when the sun's rays cascade through the window. Instead, the color turns a hue of black. His eyes are like prehistoric tar pits lying in wait for helpless animals. Mismatching the depressing scene, his nose looks somewhat Grecian, with a prominent ridge connecting each nostril. I must say his masculine jawline does not correlate with his unkempt physique; it appears more chiseled than expected. His lips are constantly pursed tightly as if he is in continuous thought, creating an unappealing look. The upper lip is thin, like a fine-tipped quill mark, and the bottom looks to have been the gluttonous one shadowing a dimpled chin peeking out from underneath.

The endeavor to look into his eyes is more difficult than expected and makes his short stature apparent. As I try to locate his gaze, I see the top of his head, and when looking down, I find it is not the most scenic view. The wig's presentation is substandard, making it difficult to conclude whether it has been improperly glued or left on for days. Either way, I'm sure of one thing: it reeks of mildew. Also, its rich brunette color doesn't genuinely match his identity. In fact, both the texture and shade do not blend with the mousy brown locks wildly adorning the sides of his temples. If the details of his wishful appearance reflect how he views himself, I will be in for a big treat. His distorted perception of his appearance might be his most outlandish character trait yet. Most of my other suitors appeared tall, and their looks matched their attitudes. In their minds, they felt their appearance justified their actions. Continuously they would treat others like rubbish because of it and society condoned their immoral behavior.

The combination of my fiancé's unappealing appearance and mismatched style provided him no wiggle room for a piss-poor personality. If he treated others without respect, he would be heinous, nothing more and nothing less. Avoiding direct eye contact with the fellow, I peer down to analyze his choice of shoes. Two black crocodile-skin boots hug his feet, each toe embellished with bizarre long fringe. Immediately I notice the bottom of his pants is unhemmed, with strings hanging from each frayed cuff. The spectacle makes him look like a mini Clydesdale. You'd think he would refrain from cutting so many corners on his wedding day of all days.

Suddenly the sound of something humming distracts me. Finding the noise perturbing to my ears, I reluctantly peruse his tacky outfit to identify what is creating the unpleasant low buzz. As the detective inside me grows closer to uncovering the culprit behind the disturbance, my soul revs with exhilaration. Well, I am enthused until my eyes land on the ratty patch of hair sticking out from his generously unbuttoned shirt. Does the man think he's a seductress? I can't conclude if he's trying too hard or just being his genuine self. The only question I find a direct answer to is the origin of the odd sound, which stems from his lungs. I've never heard a man make such an off-putting noise. He is indeed a peculiar man, one of a kind. As the noise travels from his lungs to his mouth, I follow the sound's journey until my glare finally lands on his face.

Meeting my gaze, he gawps at me like a child staring at his mother, and it takes everything in me not to exercise my first instinct of patting the top of his tiny head. I refrain from making any drastic movements and leave my eyes on his even though I find the concept of us being the only two at the altar somewhat strange. As he clears his throat again, I force myself to break away from his awkward stare to scan the room for the ceremony's officiant. Immediately I sense his eyes follow mine, and he fidgets impatiently.

It's apparent he wants to speak as I hear him gasp. "Don't worry, my love. We will be married soon enough," he states.

Each of his words makes me cringe. Masking my distaste for his social ineptitude might be my most heroic feat yet. Does he not see an issue? The gentleman sent to conduct our matrimony is missing. Is this whole thing merely a charade? As my thoughts spiral, the organist pounds the final chord. Shuddering at the lack of pitch, I turn to glare at him. The short man raises his hands to my eardrums and claps in conjunction with the song's end. I think his original motive was to build my excitement, but in truth, his actions make me spiteful.

"Bravo! Bravo!" he exclaims.

Trying to mute his speech, I pretend to ignore his theatrics and remain turned toward the musician. His lack of modesty shocks me; as the last note echoes through the church, he stands to take a bow.

"What outstanding talent," Fitz says, clapping even louder near my ear.

I shrug my right shoulder to block the sound created by his noisy paws.

"Indeed," I reply through clenched teeth.

Reluctantly I lift my hands to match his and softly clap. I support the arts, but the atrociously executed tune makes my clapping hands feel grimy. The man at the organ pushes the instrument's bench farther behind him to make way for his exit. The friction against the stone floor causes screeching sounds to rise through the arches of the vaulted ceilings. Straining to find something to appreciate, my mind grasps on to the notion that his performance has ended.

Well, that's one thing I can be thankful for.

All at once, I realize my mind may have spoken too soon. At first, I was relieved the man was done playing the ill-structured tune, but another worrying observation takes its place. Holding in a snicker, I watch his adult-sized knickers freely sway with his skipping movements. Each bounce draws attention to his polished buckle-toed shoes. The ensemble looks like it was thieved from a deceased leprechaun. His whimsical advance made my fiancé escalate his behavior to a new level of attention seeking.

"The man of the hour!" he shouts, his hands cupping his mouth to funnel the sound.

This is about to get interesting. I think with a smirk.

Fitz oddly wears jealousy on his sleeve as he watches the man bounce toward us. I can't seem to get past the idea that the musician may be just as ridiculous as my fiancé, if not more so. Wherever did he find such a similar man? I mean, did he interview many contenders for this position? So many thoughts run circles in my mind that my face turns a shade of pink as I hold back a loud giggle.

"Indeed," I say.

A single word is all I can get out while holding back my laughter. I watch as the fidgeting musician's wig shifts slightly to the side of his head, revealing a shiny bald patch. Thinking the placement looks familiar, I turn to analyze the head of my husband-to-be, and they oddly match. After one final hop of his feet, the fascinating fellow lands with a thud between us. Raising his hand to the sky, Fitz slaps his palm against the musician's back. As they laugh in unison, the blend of their voices sounds like a perfect harmony, and my thoughts spiral again, this time with outlandish ideas.

Oh, holy Christ.

I rub my eyes to zero in on what I'm seeing. Placing one hand on top of my left eye, I block half of the manly duo to get a better look and then vice versa. While I'm trying to formulate my theory, a sinister laugh echoes from the far corner behind me, and I turn around to look. As my head rotates, Fitz speaks, and my attention redirects to him.

"Brother, meet the bride. Bride, meet my brother, Franz," he says, pointing to each of us.

"You never mentioned you had a twin," I say.

"Ol' Fitz here always tries to hide me because I got all the dashing looks," the musician says.

Trying to mask my dumbfounded expression, I look at their faces again. If the musician were wigless and outfitted by the same tailor, I'm not sure they could be told apart. The two catch my look of confusion and think they have stumped me. In unison, they wrap an arm around the other's shoulders and obnoxiously laugh. Joseline chimes in and claps with glee.

"There are two of you! Isn't that something," I say.

Behind me, my shadow friend roars with laughter. As his vibrato booms, I close my eyes to regain focus, and my thoughts on the matter digress.

Why would a higher being duplicate such a horrible specimen?

Fitz, delighted by the length of my pining state, finally breaks his laughter by speaking. "I thought who better to marry us than another one of me," he says, giving me a toothy smile.

His words make my eyes bulge with disbelief. As I clench my fists, my shadow friend's laughter grows more boisterous. Closing my eyes, I center my thoughts and take a deep breath. Not favoring the feeling of being blindsided, I know I must take hold of my rising anger, and I stand in silence for a moment to maintain my composure. Suddenly my focus homes in on the sound of laughter echoing from the pews.

Them again?

I turn around, calmly looking in the direction of the laughter. My former husbands have made a grand return. Unlike my first encounter with them, their presence greatly annoys me.

I'm sure you all think this is rather amusing.

Each of their chuckles builds louder to mock me. Compressing my fists tighter, I try to quiet my building agitation. Fitz has some nerve trying to pull the wool over my eyes like this. Let me tell you, after this account, I will never take another shortcut. The shadow taught me a sickening lesson about not courting strangers through letters alone. You cannot accurately discern who is on the other end, speaking back to you through the quill and papyrus. This man standing across from me is a prime example of that, as he's the biggest con I've ever encountered. It is utterly apparent that engaging in long-distance conversation allows predators to exercise freedom when playing with others' feelings, and one can portray themselves however they like. Like carving a sculpture, the pursuer creates a fantasy for their reader about how they wish to be imagined. This only further proves my point that people can be vile.

I will only say this one more time: whoever reads my words, please learn from my mistakes and take them as an omen. Be wary that you too, can be stuck in my horrifying predicament with a conning troll or two. Never get to know a man or woman through methods where you do not first meet them in their physical form. I shall like a justified reason for my current suffering, so do not take my words in vain. Opening my eyes, I see both spitting images of the men broadly grinning back at me.

"It looks as if Mother lost her bet on you finding a bride before me," Fitz says, nudging his doppelgänger.

"Not so fast. Maybe your betrothed would prefer to marry me," Franz says with a wink.

The notion of choosing one over the other makes me want to retch.

Who raised these buffoons? I think, releasing a high-pitched giggle to distract their attention from my squirming legs.

"I fear he already has ownership over me," I say with a cough.

As Franz's face grows a drastic shade of red, it's clear he's not familiar with taking no for an answer. You may not believe this, but Fitz's triumphant win over his brother makes him even more boastful.

"Told you! Ha! She would never pick you over me. Everyone knows I'm much better looking," Fitz chides, then sticks out his tongue.

"We are identical, you twat," Franz says with a sneer.

Only my ears are privy to the heckling from the audience, and the banter makes me grin. It's like watching a two-headed circus animal performing a farcical act.

"Fight, fight, fight, fight!" the onlookers chant.

How the scene unfolds makes little sense to me; if I were to retell this account to anyone else, they might accuse me of lying. As the two little boys' blood begins to boil, I slowly take a few steps back to watch. Although I want to join in the chanting, I know silence will be my most helpful friend in this situation. Turning to Joseline, I see her nerves taking hold of her psyche. Compulsively she chews on her nails like a beaver gnawing wood. Shrugging, I lift the bottom of my dress and sit next to her in the pew.

"I've never seen them like this, miss," she says.

Her words are unreliable and hard to fathom. The brothers' competitive behavior appears to be second nature and beyond the point of healthy. Their little bodies seem to be inflicted with years of rage caged within their bones. I assume their anger stems from their parents' constantly comparing them while they were growing up or pitting them against each other for their frivolous entertainment. Fran's face seethes with rage, as he lunges for Fitz's fragile knees. They look like a duo of jesters as they wrestle. The sound of their brick-built bodies hitting the floor causes Joseline to hide her face in my lap. Forcefully I use my hands to lift her off my legs and return her to an upright position.

"Get hold of yourself, girl. You must act appropriately. Let them handle their family matters like men," I say, then turn to glare at my rowdy ex-husbands behind me.

Facing forward, Joseline sniffles and nods. "You are right, miss. My actions were inappropriate," she replies, her eyes drifting to the floor.

Joseline's gaze suddenly lifts, and she turns to survey where my eyes are fixed in order to distract herself from the chaotic scene.

"What do you see, miss?" she asks.

I smile as my mutilated husbands lift their hands to wave at me flirtatiously. Even in death, they still have charm. While the pew's inhabitants contentedly engross me, the child waves her hand in front of my face to get my attention, and I snap with frustration.

"Can't a woman have a moment to take in the scenery on her special day?" I ask.

As we glare into each other's eyes, three loud thuds resound from the front of the church. At the peak of their wrestling match, the brothers roll down the shallow three steps that lead to the altar and land on the floor in front of us.

"Fools," the deep, raspy voice whispers in my ear.

Although my friend's words make me grin, the noise of the grown men beating each other causes Joseline to fidget in her seat. Before I can turn to address the annoying tapping of her toe against the hardwood floor, she stands.

What in the world is she doing? I remain in disbelief as I watch her nervous body flinch.

"I have to do something, miss," she states. "They're going to hurt themselves."

Tired of her unbearable conduct, I embrace my indifference. "Do as you wish, child," I say, moving my hand in the air.

After spouting my words, I lose all care about the situation and opt to sit back and relax—an action I rarely have the opportunity to experience. To be truthful, I enjoy the relaxing sensation a great deal; in fact, it's refreshing. Taking a deep breath to soak in the moment's peace, I watch with amusement as Joseline sprints to break up the boys' escalating brawl. What I thought was the worst wedding ceremony I've ever participated in has pleasantly surprised me. The spectacular turn of events transpiring before my eyes makes me disregard any complaint I had over my terrible dress.

Reaching the mangled men, Joseline bends over to get their attention. Grabbing a handful of Fitz's shirt ruffles, she is forcefully thrust into the destructive tornado. I want to reiterate that the child needs to listen better to others' advice.

"Told you so," I say, chuckling.

If one could easily weed out the less agreeable from society's breeding pool, the world would be a much better place. In a matter of moments, the scene takes a gruesome turn as blood pools across the chapel floor. The mess becomes so intertwined with the trio that it's impossible to decipher to whom the bulk of the bodily fluid belongs. As Franz swings his fist to take a whack at Fitz, his wig flies into the air and lands in a puddle of gore next to a few floating teeth. Unfortunately his aim was much like his organ playing and not one of his strong suits. Unable to control his trajectory, he accidentally hits the poor chambermaid between the eyes. The sound of her skull cracking reminds me of the dream I had last night.

Wanting a better view of the festivities, I lean closer. As the brothers bash each other in rage, they inflict numerous deep gashes on each other, and vast blood loss occurs; their concussed incoherence causes them to disregard the dying maid. The single blow to her head produced incredible momentum, which caused her to collapse and her skull to smash violently against the hardwood floor. Oblivious to her unconsciousness, the boys slip in her crimson fluid as they strangle each other. The spectacle is magnificent; this is the first time anyone has put on a show for me. I angle farther forward, to the point of almost toppling to the ground.

Spurts of blood spew from Fitz's mouth as he tightens his grip around Franz's neck. "Die!" he yells, squeezing the life from his sibling's eyes.

They indeed are talented performers and deserve an ovation. Standing, I loudly clap and am pleased to hear my valiant supporters join the applause. The unwigged musician loudly releases one last gurgling breath as his limp body rolls flat on its back. In death, his eyes remain plastered open, blankly staring up at his assailant.

Although Fitz is the group's only survivor, he is in terrible shape. His face is so swollen that he can't appreciate the full extent of the destruction executed by his hands. As he strains to smile, a sizable gap, due to his missing several front teeth, is showcased, solving the mystery of the teeth on the floor. I remain a comfortable distance away as I continue to watch.

"Slip on the shit you carelessly missed," the dark voice calls from the corner.

"This is about to get even better," I say, cracking a smile and chuckle.

The grand finale is about to begin, exciting me to no end. As the lone gladiator tries to remain standing on his feet while smugly claiming victory, his shiny crocodile boots have no traction. Slipping and sliding on the immense collection of bodily fluid, his feet slide out from under him, and his arms flail to the ceiling. His landing is a perfect storm. As he's unable to catch himself to lessen the fall, the back of his skull forcefully hits the edge of the step that leads up to the altar. By the telltale sound of his bones shattering and the residual lack of movement, it's apparent his life is over. I force a moment of silence on myself to process everything I just witnessed, including the aftermath.

"Hmm," I state, folding my arms across my body.

The applause ramps up from behind me, making me turn. I'm surprised to see all my husbands give me a standing ovation for my work. Why are they proud of me? Or is this just a form of mockery? Feeling I had no part in the imbeciles' demise, I wave my hand to shoo them away. The last thing I ever imagined being called in my life is a fraud, and they're trying to make me feel like one.

"Hope, Hope, Hope, Hope," they chant.

As I scan their faces, I notice something different. Besides the original four members of my fan club, three new souls have appeared at the end of the line. Comparing each added corpse and those lying on the floor, I shrug. This occasion indeed has me at a loss for words, and though the group regards me a hero, I felt nothing of the sort. The whole situation makes me feel unfulfilled and lazy. Refusing to acknowledge the masses, I storm out of the chapel and slam the doors behind me.

The wind is refreshing against my skin, and I take time to enjoy my freedom dancing along with the breeze. As I twirl, my mind fixates on how uncomfortable the wedding dress's cheap fabric is against my skin. The itchy sensation is intolerable and drives me insane. Reaching behind my back, I frantically tear the material at the seams. All I can think about is getting this tasteless outfit away from my skin. Mania fuels my actions as swirling thoughts possess my mind. Each clinging piece of fabric makes my lungs feel suffocated, the claustrophobia making me crazed. I can't breathe. My eyes fill with tears as I let the rushing chilled air carry my screams.

As my lungs drive out the last wail, I hear the therapeutic sound of the fabric tearing within my fingertips and am overwhelmed with relief. Ripping the gown the rest of the way feels like my greatest accomplishment of the day. Once finished, I drop the poorly constructed garment to the ground, leaving myself clothed in only my corset and under slip. Feeling like a free bird, I spin in circles. At the peak of my enjoyment, my hysterical laughter is cut short by the sound of carriage wheels approaching up the rocky road.

"Shit," I say, staring down at my undressed body.

Thinking this may be the moment I'm finally caught for my actions, I run to the church to hide. A quarter of the way into my sprint, I remember I left the wedding dress on the ground, so I reversed direction to retrieve it. Snatching the material into my grip feels like a chore, and it only slows my pace as it crawls in the wind behind me. As I escape into the chapel, I shut the door and notice the commotion is gone. The only corpses left to haunt me are the three on the floor near the altar. With disgust, I look at the ripped gown in my hands and walk with purpose to the blood-soaked bodies, tossing the material on top of them to hide the gruesome scene.

"Take this with you to hell," I shout as I spit on them.

I then quietly turn back around and calmly tiptoe to the door to peek outside. Before cracking it open, my shaking hand clutches the locket around my neck for support, and the cold metal warms my heart. A familiar voice hums a soothing melody from the corner of the chapel, and without turning my head, I hum the tune in unison with my shadow friend. As my racing heart calms, I let my hand crack open the door to look for the trespasser, and the sound of a steed's whinny makes my eyes widen. Opening the door farther, I see the familiar black carriage waiting for me and dramatically roll my eyes.

"Thank God," I mutter.

The sight of my savior makes me feel like I'm floating on a cloud while exiting the chapel. As I race across the field, the unmistakable aroma of the piss-laden driver provides me with an odd sense of happiness.

"Let's get the fuck out of here, chap," I call to him as I move to the carriage door.

I'm not expecting a response, as I've never heard the driver speak. During each of our lengthy rides, I attributed his silence to being mute. As I place my hand on the carriage's door handle, I notice my trunk with my belongings has already been strapped to the back for my current travel.

"Now that is what I call first-rate service," I say.

The driver laughs and my hand freezes.

Guess he isn't mute after all. I shrug and let out a snicker.

After taking a moment to shake away the icy shiver from my skin, I hoist myself into the carriage, and my eyes are met with a fabulous imported silk ensemble displayed on the seat.

"Impeccable," I say with a grin as I shut the door.

As the carriage commences its bumpy journey, my fingers caress the richness of the new fabric.

"Now this is what I call a proper gown," I murmur.

Admiring the well-constructed dark-navy silk taffeta with decadent lace accenting each pleat, I confirm that it transcends all expectations. I've never seen such a magnificent dress—soothing to the touch, the fabric feels like butter against my frame. As I relax in the carriage, I know I'm ready for my next adventure. Placing my hand on the seat cushion next to me, I feel a palm cup mine, sending a wave of warmth from my fingertips to my elbow.

"Hello, my friend," I say.

Although no one replies, I know I'm not alone, and the comfort is enough to last me a lifetime. Preparing for a lengthy journey, I allow my eyes to close. Everything seems effortless as I listen to the carriage wheels tread on the ground, the melodic sound cleansing my mind.

"See you on the other side, my cherished friend," I whisper before drifting off to sleep.

Chapter Eight

TALL, DARK, AND HANDSOME

The ride's lengthy duration does not treat me with the typical kindness I've experienced before, and my dreams wear heavily on my psyche. Once again, I find the lids of my weary eyes reliving my family's gruesome massacre. One could say the thought of my body being pulled toward the table's centerpiece is alluring to me. Having experienced the hypothetical scenario night after night, I've come to enjoy the inclusivity of sitting around the dining room table together. After being subjected to my family, in both deceased and living states, I've grown fond of the dream, preferring them to have muted tongues. This preference, which I've grown to love, makes the present scenario ideal for me, and I've found the only gripe I have involving the encounter is the evolution of the dream's contents.

Earlier in our time together, I elucidated the dream's details that I could recount. Since then, the nightly happenings have grown more gruesome, with a shifting storyline. Rather than leave my skin unscathed, the nightmare feeds me a vague depiction of my death. Initially I took the change as an exciting omen, the light leaving my pupils not acting as a prediction of my demise but rather a creative way for my shadow friend to teach me not to trust others. I believed I would remain safe as long as the hard exterior protecting my soft soul remained intact and as long as I never lowered my guard to the outside world. I can't say precisely when my perspective regarding the information fed to me changed, but it did.

My newly enhanced dream gave additional details, bringing about a transformation to my vision. Rather than being cast as the massacre's lone survivor, it thrust me into Daniel Manley's stylish shoes to gain clarity. Placing my hands on each lifeless body was therapeutic and freeing. At the time of their slayings, I do not know how he stopped himself amid the acts of violence. If I were put into the moment of each separate killing, I honestly wouldn't possess the same self-control. Dealing with each heinous personality, I would have made every face unrecognizable.

Pacing on top of the dining room table, I gaze down at each of the mutilated bodies and gleefully smile. As I scan the dining room chairs, my eyes fixate on the one Daniel bound me to, and we have switched positions. He patiently sits before me with a devious smirk while one of his legs delicately rests on top of the other knee as he waits for the show to begin. His manicured hands wrench together before he reaches to the table to pluck a row of grapes off a silver platter.

As I fixate on the way he scalps the grape's skin with his teeth, I suddenly detect that my feet are unable to take another step. A moment later, I feel a tightening sensation around my neck. As my breath is taken from my lungs, I hear Daniel's loud cackle. Though my vision grows fuzzy from the lack of oxygen, I can see the outline of his figure staring past me from the corner of the room.

"I told you she was just like me," he says, tossing another grape into his mouth.

The laughter coincides with my fading vision and concludes the dream. The thought of Daniel even saying we are of the same species perturbs me. His speech was a lie: we are entirely two different creatures. He is a monster who enjoys killing for pleasure, while I'm cleaning up society for the benefit of others. For that reason, I refuse to acknowledge how any of our motives or actions are analogous. If someone ignorantly thinks my words are mush and our motives are similar, they are welcome to compare us further. They would identify many other differences when placing us in a side-by-side comparison. One may point out that an obvious differentiating factor is our intellect. All of you who have seen him have witnessed him use his suave persona to cover up his stupor. I am by far more well-read and knowledgeable about worldly matters than he.

Although it's clear Daniel and I are nothing alike, I still can't stop myself from lying awake after each dream, wondering why he believes we're so alike. Thinking from Daniel's ungodly perspective, I admit he could squeeze out a few common points of interest. We both have identified loathing qualities in the family I was born into, and we bask in the finer things in life. Besides those commonalities, I can't seem to piece together any other correlations, yet he still haunts my thoughts. I know I'm missing something because

I can't shake his image. Until I find the blind spot in my mind, I will patiently wait for the secret's grand unveiling.

The sound of snapping horse's reins jolts me awake. As my mouth releases a yawn, I stretch my upper body to the sky. I have grown fond of traveling and the time it grants me to reflect on my experiences—meditation is crucial for healing and for purging all negativity from your being. Before peeking out the window at my new surroundings, I take a long deep breath to center my thoughts. Again, I hear the reins crack as they slap the horse's rear. As the terrain becomes smoother beneath the carriage wheels, my curiosity takes over.

As I gaze out the small oblong window, I see dawn rising around us. I find the tainted imagery of the surrounding street lit by ornate gas lamps eerily beautiful. Each storefront's glass window showcases fine-looking dresses highlighted by the windowpane's reflections of orange-gray tones. Unlike the other small towns I've visited, this one appears more significant and industrial. Most of the buildings have chimneys pushing out soot for the morning's rolling fog to carry away. Even with the smoke plumes discharging into the stagnant air, the main street maintains a kempt and swept appearance.

My eyes squint, seeking to discover any peculiarities in the terrain, permitting me to get a sharper view of the upcoming side streets. The dark passageways sprout from the primary route, obscured from view like concealed children a parent is embarrassed about. Due to poor lighting, all the adjoining alleys are ominously hidden from the onlooker's central line of sight. In the shadows of a single side street, a malnourished child rummages through a pile of trash, and the spectacle causes sickness to plague my stomach. I know the responsibility and decision lie on both parents, but I can't help wonder why they chose to have a child when they had no means to care for it properly. I pondered the same thing when my parental figures constantly neglected me.

Why have a child if you have no love or care to give? The notion still haunts me.

Since we are within the depths of reflection, let's take the analysis a step further. Amassing anguish on top of severe neglect, imagine growing up in a town with drastic class differences, a place without a middle class, where only the wealthy and impoverished reside. If you were unfortunately born into the latter group, not only would you have no support from the ones who brought you into the world, but also there would be nowhere to turn for assistance. Since the rich are primarily apathetic toward the difficulties of the poor, and without the option of accessing the more sympathetic middle class, you'd be left without an opportunity to attain food or shelter other than digging through rubbish and huddling inside alley doorways. With no solution at your fingertips, every day you'd wake up wondering if your life would ever improve. Those who have the financial means to help will not, and the economically disadvantaged want to help but cannot. The level of hopelessness would be atrocious.

It is most upsetting how society claims to rally for the oppressed classes but never forms a method to implement their promises of change. Listen closely, for I will express why the rich love to side with those who are financially beneath them. It is all a grand scheme to keep the socioeconomic levels passively intact. The only motive for upholding social divides is to serve the affluent class's political agendas and ensure those individuals retain power. If they were to solve all the world's deeper societal issues, they would have no one left to look to them for solutions, no reason to lead, and nothing to prove their worth. Societal autonomy would weaken their supremacy and eradicate their importance.

Wanting to turn from the depressing topic to happy thoughts, I redirect my attention to the beautiful material draped on my body then to the cabin's glass portal. Typically, when moving to a new location, I awake from my slumber just as we arrive at my destination, but this time is different; I am alert and able to survey each fascinating detail as we pass through town. Like a child in a toy shop, I am captivated by the architecture.

Reluctant to miss a single detail, I shift my glance to the window on the opposite side of the carriage. I notice an attractive street lined with houses whose exteriors are especially appealing. The magnificent style is something I haven't witnessed before; my eyes were virgin to the architectural elegance. Now hone your detective skills and ready yourself for a vital reference that hints to the era of these houses. The closest comparison I can summon to describe the whimsical street is the Moulin Rouge. Though I haven't witnessed it in person, I have heard rumors depicting the newly opened realm many deem unrestrained and found that the imagery thrust me into wild fantasies on many occasions. Some nights I stood in front of the mirror, envisioning running away and picturing what it would be like to live as a cabaret performer. I imagined performing in front of large cheering crowds. Every flawless can-can kick of my leg would display glimpses of my bare skin, hypnotizing each gawping onlooker.

Engulfed by the magnificent spectacle outside, I slide my body closer to the glass and press my hands against the frame, my pupils awestruck by all the sensations. Colorful scarves wave from each window, dancing in the breeze as a fiddler sits on the street corner, tapping his foot to the beat played from the strokes of his rosined bow. He smiles at a woman with red curly hair who dances to the music. She appears free, and I find her confidence admirable.

The material on her frame shows the position of wealth she has gained from her profession. Drawing attention to her hourglass physique, she wears an outfit showcasing wild ruffles and a large crimson red bustle matching the color of her curls. In her hand, she spins a closed decorative parasol. She lifts her petticoat to kick her leg and show her bloomers before giving her final curtsy. The fiddler claps to commend her energetic performance as she pushes her cleavage together and takes a bow. Although I know they won't hear my praise, I compulsively clap.

"The organist should be here to take lessons," I say with a snicker.

The woman's body swivels toward my moving carriage as if responding to my applause, and her eye winks. Embarrassment sweeps over my bones, and I pull myself away from the window to hide.

How did she catch my glance? I think, panicking.

Still, her charisma intrigues me. When I made eye contact with her, a spark of energy sifted through my body, and I felt alive. Moving my eyes back to the window, I observe her walk farther down the street toward a red-painted door. I find the unique entry color pulls at my soul's strings; the presentation sets it apart from the rest of the surrounding businesses. With a single crack of the whip, the driver conducts the black stallion pulling our carriage to move faster, and the street leaves my sight.

Even though the red-haired woman and the door are far in the distance, both still captivate my mind. Maybe it's because I wish to live a life with less responsibility. Her expectations of her clients' behavior would be minimal, unlike mine, where I'm forced to deal with heinous wealthy men who try to cross me. Often I feel as though the brunt of the world's weight rests on my shoulders. As each of my traumas continues to build upon another, I find it difficult to function in society and at times wish to crawl into permanent hibernation. Not having to outwit another man would be refreshing. How wonderful it would be to enter every situation knowing the expectation would just be to live and be. If I lived the life of the red-haired woman, society would harbor little expectation for me and me for it.

Accompanying my rambling thoughts, the carriage bobbles, then suddenly halts. The horse leading our way rears to the sky before stomping each metal shoe against the stone path. Abruptly my mind jars with spinning ideas regarding the horse's disruptive motion.

Who is interrupting my pleasant thoughts? Rage fills my toes then makes its way to each fingertip.

Ignoring my frustration, the carriage remains stationary. Trying to stay patient, I wait to see if our journey will recommence. In the thick of the moment, the last thing I want to do is cause a dramatic scene in front of the town's residents, whom I aim to seduce. Releasing a deep breath, I steady my quivering palms against the edge of the seat. When the carriage remains still, however, my legs become restless. Losing all patience, I peer out the window to determine what is holding us up. To my disappointment, my vision is obstructed.

I roll my eyes. "Of course there's a blind spot."

I stare at my bare hands with discontentment. If I want to be privy to the obstacle, I must open the door and present myself appropriately; the skin on my hands must be covered. Claustrophobia sets in as I impatiently search the surrounding seats for a pair of gloves, crawling on my knees to peer in every nook. Just as I'm about to claim defeat, I sit back on the cushioned bench and spot a pair of matching long navy gloves waving from the shadow seated across from me. The breathtaking sight makes my lips quiver with a smile and turns my body warm.

"You're always one step ahead, my friend," I say.

My hand stretches for the gloves, and just as it touches the edge of the shadow, something forcefully jams the tips of my fingers. Reacting from the shock of the pain, I retract my stunned hand to my side and fall back into my seat. Until that moment, I hadn't experienced a single negative tendency or punishment from my shadow friend, and the hurtful behavior made my trust waver.

Is the mysterious being not happy with my recent actions? Did I do something improper? My mind reels with racing thoughts.

Having completed everything requested, I'm bewildered by my friend's lack of appreciation. Frantically I stare at the floor, replaying each of my last steps to determine where I may have shown disrespect to the shadow, and out of my peripheral vision, I glimpse a darkened genderless figure. The presence makes my teeth chatter.

Clenching my fists, I clear my throat to speak. "If you're trying to frighten me, it won't work."

Something feels uneasy and different about the situation. Before I can take a breath, a deep devious laugh comes from the dark silhouette, the sound weighing heavily in the cabin like a dense morning fog. Immediately the air surrounding my breath becomes stagnant and thick. Pungent smog fills the compartment like a gas chamber, piquing my curiosity. The smell of smoke from a burning pipe entices my nostrils and brings me a disturbing sense of comfort.

"Scare you? Ha!" The mysterious figure responds with a cackle.

The odor from the burning tobacco becomes stronger under my nose. Trying to place the familiarity, I close my eyes to visualize my last memory regarding the distinct aroma. As my lids open, I'm startled to see my fourth husband Robert, perched in front of me, smoking his pipe.

Oh, bloody hell, there he is. I try to withhold my irritation.

This must be what I get for choosing narcissistic men as targets for marriage. Even in death, they still become jealous if their story gets less attention than the rest. Honestly, I've thought about my summary of his presence in my life enough, but the sight of his body wearing the characteristic outfit tells me otherwise. The ivory coattails on his stiff body are the same ones he wore the day of our last encounter, and no, it was not a special occasion. He perpetually wore ivory as a peacocking statement and treasured the town's socialites addressing his clothing choices in daily conversation.

Contradicting his stark discolored white skin, the veins bulge in his eyes as he blows smoke in my face and chuckles. His curled mustache is villainous in appearance, and his teeth remain discolored from the blood he coughed up when dying. When planning his death, I wanted to play with the idea of family tradition, so, like his father, I felt it fitting to give him a similar dose of the poppy mixture to exterminate him.

Continuing to puff his pipe, he tilts his head toward me. "I know what you did," he says, wearing a smug look.

His voice radiates a weird combination of dried gravel and humming calmness, and the frivolous information he believed necessary to share unnerves me.

"Whatever do you mean?" I reply, my eyes drifting up and meeting his.

His pupils stand black and soulless. My irises feel dry as a ring of smoke floats into the center of each cornea. Although his pathetic game is to intimidate me, I will do everything in my power not to let his pitiable attempts affect me. The burning sensation causes my lips to smirk as I convert my discomfort to pleasure and try to ignore his presence. Refocusing my attention, I scan the area surrounding his seat for my gloves and prepare for my escape.

He reaches underneath his roosted body, pulls out the gloves, and tauntingly holds them in front of his face. "Looking for these?" he says with a mocking cackle.

Anger flushes my skin. Lunging across the cabin, I snatch the gloves from his ash-stained fingers. "Give me those before you spoil them!" I demand.

As I slip each delicate glove onto my hands, without breaking eye contact I glare daggers through his soul.

"You do realize the voice you lean so heavily on does not differ from the rest of us?" he states, inhaling smoke from the black pipe.

I find each of his condescending words infuriating. Who is he to condemn another? He did not stray far from his father's tendencies, and regardless of their similarities, his father continuously vocalized the man's worthlessness. Because the apple didn't fall far from the tree, I feel their twinning narratives fitting, and he should consider himself lucky his termination took longer than expected. His death would have commenced sooner if it weren't for the delay with the postal service delivering my letters to husband number five. Instead of being grateful for his prolonged fate, he seems to have taken the act as a homage to my deep-seated feelings for him. The ridiculousness of his misguided thoughts makes me chuckle.

Primly I adjust my gloves. "You don't say,"

My mocking demeanor chips away at his helpful facade. Unable to hide his anger, his face takes on a rosy hue. Still pretending to ignore him, I feel my heart race as I move my body toward the door. Unfortunately he's blocking the exit with his decayed hands.

"Move aside," I tell him.

He flashes me a grin. "Don't be a prude."

His chauvinistic categorization tosses me into a flashback of our nights together. After a bout of heavy drinking, he'd smoke a pipe in his study until boredom set in, and like clockwork, he'd wait for the sun to set before making the lightless trek to my quarters. Once he was hovering over my body, he'd wake me by blowing smoke rings into my eyes. I still find the odor of his breath triggers my body to shut down from the extensive trauma he bestowed upon me. Some nights were so dreadful that I debated whether to give up on my life's purpose altogether, and more often than not, his sadistic treatment made me want to fall into a permanent slumber. If it weren't for my shadow friend reminding me of my worth, my soul would have remained lost in the suffering. The resilience I built is what kept me going day after day, and I believe husband number four and his father were put into my path to test my strength.

The sight of his hands continuing to block the exit feeds the anger inside me. "Move," I repeat through clenched teeth.

He waves his hand in front of the door to mock my frustration.

Why is the shadow not doing anything to stop this atrocity?- The notion confuses me.

"It is obvious you only wanted my money; you do not differ from any other gold-digging prospect I could have chosen," he says with a chuckle.

His words make my jaw tighten. In no way did I expect him to have a revelation after death, but his lacking consciousness of the horrible things he put me through night after night drives me mad. He blames me instead of accepting the karma from his atrocious abuse. He doesn't consider the potential repercussions of torturing others, and his seething frustration tells me he has no desire in his core for change.

"Of course I am. I'm most definitely different from the rest—I killed you," I reply with a smirk.

Watching him spiral in his simple frustration sparks me to stay my gloved hand on the door handle. "Oh, dear, it appears the cat's got your tongue," I say, then the knob.

Just as my fingers finish twisting the metal, someone beats me to it and flings the door open from the other side. Not expecting the door's release, my body's momentum continues in the direction of my departure and helplessly tumbles. As I fall from the carriage, my fourth husband chuckles. Preparing for the harsh impact of the cobblestones, I squeeze my eyes shut. Just as I think I'm nearing the ground, a pair of solid arms cradle the weight of my body and I'm confident my shadow friend saved me.

Cracking open my eyes, I peer up to thank my savior, but the face looks nothing as expected. The arms holding my limp body belong to a man tall in stature with dark features. Even though I've never witnessed the shadow take on a human form, I know this man was not it. With his olive-toned skin and green eyes, he looks like a tall glass of trouble. His facial features are perfectly proportioned, with a day's stubble fashionably gracing his cleft chin. Everything about him screams temptation, in a Jack the Ripper sort of way. As I gaze up at him, his mesmerizing eyes analyze my face.

"Are you alright?" he asks.

"I am now," I reply with a flirtatious grin.

"I must say I've never seen such a graceful dismount," he says with a seductive smile.

My face turns flush from embarrassment, and I sheepishly cover my eyes. As my hands darken my vision, I have a flashback of the last suitor the shadow put in my path. The image of each strand of his pubescent chest hair makes my shoulders tremble, and the realness of the memory makes me question the attractive man's existence. Maybe this is hell, and as soon as I open my eyes I'll be greeted from my dream state by the troll from the chapel.

Wanting to see if husband number five has replaced the statuesque Adonis, I reluctantly force open the fingers over my eyes. As I peek through the slit, I see the stranger's chiseled jawline and smell a whiff of his cologne. His scent has a remnant sensation of holiday cinnamon and pine. The knowledge that he exists makes my eyes widen.

He looks concerned. "Do you feel ill?" he asks, helping me to my feet.

As my weight returns to a standing position, I see the carriage from the corner of my eye and recognize husband number four staring at me from the cabin's shadowy depths. Being dramatic, he lifts the hand holding the pipe to wave, and ash drops to the floor of the carriage as he deviously smirks. I glare icy daggers at him to express my disgust for his actions. Quickly reaching forward, I slam the carriage door shut, and the sight washes away his smirk. Using the polished door, I take a moment to gaze at my reflection and check my appearance. I pinch my cheeks to reset my attitude and turn my apples a healthy shade of rose. As I clear my throat with a high-pitched tone, I gracefully swivel my body back to face my new suitor.

"I dare say I am much better now," I respond.

He laughs at my eccentric nature, his eyes smoldering to show his interest. I commence my glance at the toes of his polished black wingtip shoes, then gradually work my way up to his face. His body appears quite fit under his perfectly tailored coat and tails. As I notice the black satin trim around his lapel and small buttons made from mother-of-pearl, it becomes apparent by the flawless details that the man has wealth. During my extensive visual excavation, I eye up his bare ring finger. While he clutches his decorative gold embellished bird-shaped cane, his teeth lightly bite his lip as he smiles.

"That is jolly good! I'm so happy you are well," he says.

I return a flirtatious grin to his kind words. Although I find myself entranced by our time together, I can't shake the thought that someone is watching us, and nerves set in. Worried he might discover the unwelcome passengers in my carriage, I swiftly devise a ploy.

"Are you traveling far?" I ask, pointing to his grand carriage, which stopped in front of mine.

Three dappled gray steeds with perfectly braided manes lead his transport. The cabin's exterior is crafted of mahogany with ornate brass accents. The design appears so rich that any king would be content to take a ride in it. Squinting around him, I peer into the open door and see the plush bright-purple interior. Following my stare, he looks at the driver, who sits patiently waiting for him with the horses' reins in hand. The man is dressed in a velvet baroque coat and knickers that perfectly match the carriage's majestic interior.

"I'm just returning from holiday," he says, raising a hand to acknowledge the patient driver.

As soon as I determine that my plan to distract him has worked, I glance back to my carriage window. The compartment has grown darker, and I sense my shadowy friends' irritation. But I don't care; it's fair to experience happiness in an organic interaction for the first time; my friend is selfish for trying to seize that from me.

"Stop it," I whisper, curling my fists into a ball.

The ethos behind my two words causes the gentlemen's head to snap toward me. My posture straightens to compensate for my panicking thoughts.

Oh, dear God, how will I explain my words? I think, putting on a fake smile.

"Pardon my distraction. Did you say something?" he inquires.

"Oh, yes. I was merely calling to my driver," I reply.

Confusion blankets his face as I attempt to feed my lie. All the while, not knowing the handsome gentlemen's name distracts me.

"Driver!" I command, clapping my hands in the air.

Trying to calm my frazzled energy, the man tries to help fill my loss for words. "Your carriage driver is the reason I stopped my travel home," he says.

"Oh?" I reply, distractedly peering around the carriage, searching for the driver.

"He looks immensely similar to a driver my family once had. I know it's not of great importance, but he was like a second father to me, especially after my father's passing. I'm sure it's just my mind playing tricks."

He cannot possibly be referring to the man who smells of day-old piss, I think with disgust.

His eyes look dewy from reminiscing, and for the first time in a while, I feel troubled by someone's heartfelt sorrow. The sincerity behind his mourning is refreshing to me.

"I admit his loyalty to me is fairly new, so he could be the same driver you speak of," I say, placing a hand on his shoulder.

The hopeful gleam in his eyes created by my words is endearing.

"Shall we take a look?" I ask.

Leading him to the front of my carriage, I conduct my one good deed of the day, but what we find comes as a shock to both of us. The fellow has fled with my coach's only horse.

Bloody hell, I think, staring blankly at the man.

The thought makes the blood in my veins boil, and I want to take back all the praise I've ever given the man. Stunned and angry, I can't do anything other than stare dumbfoundedly at the empty seat.

"It appears your driver fled with the steed," he says.

My foot stomps with frustration, and my breath quickens with panic. Before speaking another word, the gentleman changes the subject to calm my rising emotions.

"Did you have far to travel?" he asks.

Shrugging, I think swiftly on my feet, my mind fashioning a viable story to spout. "That is a brilliant question with a rather fascinating answer. When I desire to take a holiday, I routinely play this enthralling game where my packed luggage is loaded in a waiting carriage, and I instruct my driver to surprise me with a new location."

"I see," he says.

"It worked swimmingly in the past, but like most things, I realize now, there are trials and tribulations," I say with a nervous laugh as I pace.

"I have a brilliant idea to turn this humdrum mood around. Why don't you stay at my estate? There is ample room. Usually I have a ward to look after, but the estate is quite empty, and the house has been unsettlingly silent with him away at boarding school. You can be my guest of honor until this is sorted out," he says, using his hands to express his excitement.

Again I scan the carriage to look for any sign of the driver or horse. Seeing neither, I refrain from looking in the carriage window and decide my fate for myself.

"That's very kind of you, sir," I reply with a smile.

"No need for formalities. My name is David," he says, extending his hand.

I allow him to provide a formal introduction, smirking at his tender, light kiss to the back of my hand. Something about him differs from others I have dealt with, and I've never been so comfortable around another.

"Mine is Hope," I respond.

"What a lovely name," he states, his eyes smoldering.

The look he gives me makes my heartbeat quicken. From all the books I've read over the years, this situation seems to mimic a storyline with deep flares of romance. Now, I don't believe in the rubbish of soul mates, but I find our connection different. Something about our interaction feels familiar, as if we've met many times before.

What is this feeling inside? I think, panicking.

The appearance of his face made my nerves fluster. My heart raced and fluttered in a state of panic when his steady hand extends yet again to take mine.

"Shall we?" he asks.

Letting each of his words settle into my ears, I take a moment of pause before making a final decision.

"We shall," I reply with a giggle.

Lightly holding his hand, I follow his lead to his carriage. The sounds of snoring echo from the carriage hand, who sits manning the horses' reins.

"Fredrick!" he shouts with a snap of his fingers.

The driver's head jerks alert at the sound of his words, causing his hands to tighten the reins; in unison with the tug, the three beautiful horses release whinnies. "Yes, sir," he says, his eyes scanning the area to reorient himself.

"She's traveling with us, so you must fetch her trunk," David states excitedly.

Fredrick nods as he secures the reins to a brass holder. He then hops from his position and hurries to the back of the black cabin to untie my trunk.

David and I turn to watch.

"You just have the single piece of luggage?" he inquires, motioning to the sweaty driver.

I nod. "Yes. I prefer to travel light."

He nods and smiles. "I always admire a woman of little vanity," he says, then squeezes my hand.

His reaction brings out a bashful response in me. My face turns red, and I'm at an unusual loss for words. Relinquishing my guard, I look toward the man unloading my things and catch a glimpse through the window. From the outside, the window looks pitch-black and sorrowful. Even though I feel called to return, I redirect my attention and ignore my feelings of guilt. With a last heave, Fredrick finishes unloading the chest.

"Is this everything?" he shouts at us.

"Sure is. Lucky for you, she's a light traveler!" David shouts back with a laugh.

As the driver struggles to carry the solidly built trunk toward us, we turn to look at our awaiting ride.

"I swear you won't regret this," David says with a playful wink.

During our walk to his carriage, I take one lasting look at my shadow friend. "Good riddance," I whisper.

The harsh words falling from my lips cause my heart to plummet to the pit of my stomach. I just left everything I've ever known as home and am taking a risk on a stranger. Deep down, I know the potential ghoulish fate I might suffer due to my shadow friend's devious temperament. Still, I'm willing to face all possible repercussions for my impulsive decision. Between my experience in the chapel and husband number four invading my carriage ride, it has quickly become apparent that the mysterious being took advantage of me. If I continued on the same path of living to please another, I think the haunting would break me.

David turns to look at the carriage and plays along. "Good riddance," he says with a laugh.

Tightly squeezing my hand, he enthusiastically leads me to the door of his carriage. When he releases his grip from my hand, I watch his hand clasp the handle. As the hatch on the door clicks, the aching sensation lifts from my shoulders. Quickly he pulls the door wide open and extends his hand to help me in.

"Your chariot awaits, my lady," he states with a regal demeanor.

Lightly touching my hand to his, I enter without a second thought. I don't bother taking another glance toward the past I left behind; I left it in the dust for a reason.

Chapter Nine

IT'S ONLY A SPIDER

Before the devilishly handsome stranger can completely shut the door behind us, the carriage jolts forward. The momentum from the horses' energetic pull shoves me back in my seat and makes him take a position beside me. I think the severity of my new reality sets in at once because I'm at a loss for words when looking at the gentleman who saved me. My biggest fear is buyer's remorse for my newly chosen path. There's no turning back; the shadow would never trust me the same again. The reality of my choices creates a clambering sensation in the bones of my knees, causing them to clank together like cymbals. My breathing becomes disturbingly shallow as I panic over the variety of ways the shadow could make me suffer for my decision.

Moving to the corner of my seat, I brace my palms against the two walls beside me for stability. As my spine presses harder against the backrest, I take a moment to collect myself and appreciate my panoramic view of the interior. Knowledge of one's setting is imperative when facing the possibility of an incursion. If the shadow figure were to combat my impulsivity and implement an attack, I would want to recognize all my surroundings to protect myself better. Since I've never before gone against my friend's wishes, I must prepare for anything and everything. Clueless about what the mysterious being is capable of, I must be ready for the possibility of a dramatic uprising. Allowing my eyes to focus intensely, I frantically scan every available nook and cranny.

As my eyes swiftly make their way from left to right, I glimpse my new travel companion and come to a monumental discovery. David doesn't hide his expressions well and, by his snicker, makes it undeniably clear that my skittish behavior amuses him. Honestly, his reaction might be one of disbelief. His schoolboy tone started in earnest the moment I agreed to enter his carriage. Customarily, a cultivated woman wouldn't do such a thing, especially without knowing the gentleman's character. Let me restate the previous remark with a bit more clarity: the occurrence is not generally tolerated but is considered acceptable when a woman becomes part of a marital arrangement. It is common for women to enter a coach with a stranger after being forced into a permanent contract with a man they have only met briefly if they are lucky. Although he doesn't know it yet, the inside joke surrounding our situation revolves around him. I'm not the victim—he's the one potentially in danger, not I. Even if he's smuggling away many personal secrets, I will bet sizable sums of money I still have more skeletons hiding in my closet.

Perhaps if he had taken a moment to learn more about me or had seen the figure holding my psyche hostage, his inclination to extend his gracious invitation would not have arisen. Yes, I'm confident his infatuation with me would dissipate if he knew about the entity who tormented me day after day. Sincerely, when noticing the metaphorical fork in the road ahead, I thoroughly weighed the two paths I could take, and his luster won me over. Besides his impeccable physical appeal, I find him a much better option for a travel companion than my heinous fourth husband. Anyone trapped in my predicament would have chosen the same.

When David clears his throat to get my attention, I pivot my upper body to acknowledge him. "I must let you in on a grave secret," he quietly states, holding a finger to his lips.

My eyes grow wide, and immediately I wonder if this is when this gentleman will offload his hidden baggage.

Oh, God, please don't say you've killed someone too, I think, trying to maintain my composure.

"My driver is an agreeable man, but sometimes I fear that he may be a con with his lack of proficiency at his craft. Hopefully you aren't prone to motion sickness," he says with a casual shrug.

Never having been around anyone who tries to lighten the mood with comedic tones stymies me, and my ignorance inhibits me from correctly deciphering his inflection. Fixating on his detailed expressions, I watch a smirk break across his face, confirming my suspicion that he's trying to be funny. Swiftly I switch up my serious energy to match his carefree nature and allow myself to laugh at his statement.

At the end of my hysterics, my lips part to expose a smile. "Don't worry. They made my stomach of iron," I say, my hand playfully rubbing my belly.

David's eyes follow the motion of my hand on my stomach, and the flirtatiousness of my response makes him smile. It's odd to admit so soon, but something about him allows me to enjoy a sense of normalcy I've never experienced before. In the short time I've known him, he's allowed me to unapologetically be my authentic self without a question or second thought. From each of his gleeful mannerisms, I can tell he's smitten with me, and judging by how he fidgets, my presence clearly makes him nervous. The feeling isn't one-sided; in fact, it is quite mutual.

As he opens his mouth to give a witty reply, however, he freezes. Trying again to summon a stream of coherent words, his lips meet his command with a dry stutter, and an air of embarrassment sweeps over his face. The mortified expression shown through his demeanor makes our turbulent trials even, and together we share a moment of silence before bursting into empathetic laughter.

I allow the instant's happiness to engulf me as I experience the novel act of carefree living. The confidence in me that his smile provides makes me feel invincible. At once, the joyous sensation is all too familiar, and I spend a moment placing the emotion. Everything about the intoxicating energy comes to me in flashbacks. It is the same euphoria I encountered when ridding the world of the evildoers the shadow put in my path. Since the beginning of our friendship, the shadow has expressed that the same joy would only exist upon my completion of specified tasks, so you can imagine how the lack of correlation took me by surprise. I questioned the validity of each memory and my friend's intentions.

After all, what if my suffering wasn't dependent on my friend's advice and my happiness could come from a shared feeling with someone else? An aura of loneliness overtakes me as I ponder the validity of my life's purpose.

The start of my new journey has shown me I can share myself with another without repudiation. He seemed to possess none of the characteristics I had previously identified to be deterrents in situations such as this.

How is this stranger able to prove all my prior assumptions wrong?

His condescending nature toward the facade of gentility challenges everything I've been living for. The compiling enlightenment surrounding my life's journey wears on my psyche, and David's presence, even the awkward moments, makes facing my life's upheaval frustratingly resemble a fool's errand. Everything always seems to come in the force of twos, and as quickly as I sensed the happiness bestowed upon me, a contradicting wave of self-resentment overrides my joy. My prior actions of killing my spouses now weighs heavily on my subconscious. Unable to stop every ounce of my self-worth from exiting the top of my skull, I'm left a shell of a person, a pointless fraud who doesn't deserve his affection.

Like clockwork, the shape of a shadow figure forms in the carriage's corner; little by little, its growing stealth feeds off the internalized war happening inside me. My anticipation of my friend's arrival causes my body to tense, trapping me in the closing walls of the carriage. Immediately my limbs compulsively go rogue and squirm without being provoked, giving the shadow more vitality. In a panic, I shift my gaze to the nearby window to look away from the culprit; that's when I spot the mastermind behind the terror, a passing lamppost. Quickly I force my fear to the back of my mind, place a smile on my face, and direct my attention to the man hosting our journey.

"How much longer is our ride?" I ask.

"Roughly an hour, give or take, depending on a few elements," he says, peering out the window.

While his attention drifts, the shadow continues to build in the corner, and I push my body against my seat to escape.

"Hope," a dark voice melodically whispers.

Trying to ignore the force attempting to take over my happiness, I sit upright and turn toward the window. I hoped if I neglected the being, it might leave to find another.

"You think you can choose him over me?" the deep voice asks.

The statement causes my palms to become clammy and profusely sweat through my gloves. All at once, the temperature in the cabin lowers to that of a harsh winter. The interior is so cold that it could produce mountains of snow with a bit of precipitation if given the opportunity. As I slow my breathing, my eyes shift to the frost forming on my damp hands. A clouded indentation of my breath remains in the air from my exhalation, and ice crystals grow from the massive amounts of condensation forming on the fingertips of my gloves.

What do you want from me? I think, attempting to thaw my palms on the lap of my dress.

"The answer is quite simple," the voice states.

My eyes widen at the entity's response to my statement. The sound produced by the dark, profound cackling voice saturates the cabin like a bottomless stew boiling over the scorching edge of a pot. Each of the being's seething words is laden with wrath and makes my skin crawl. Convinced the rage will eventually cease, I'm surprised by the light tickling flutter of something scurrying underneath the right sleeve of my dress. Slowly the tiny prickle migrates up my arm, causing my heart to stop. Meeting my wit's end, I cannot take the never-ending torment another second longer, and I cave to the whims of my paranoia.

The sight of the right cuff of my sleeve moving makes my arm flinch. Rubbing my eyes with my left hand, I try to clear my vision to get a second look. Even with a fresh gaze, I witness the material undulating as if something is stuck underneath and trying to escape. Overwhelmed by the ongoing torment of my shadow friend, my mind creates a rush of sheer terror that floods my bones and fills my eyes with water. Clenching my jaw to fight the oncoming tears, I observe the thing persist in its crawl under my sleeve. As the material shifts on my wrist, my limb stiffens with paralyzing fear. The absence of my friend's words is perturbing, and I try not to fixate on the mysterious being who hides in the shadows while waiting for the other shoe to drop.

The sudden awareness of movement against my earlobe causes my shoulder to shrug. "You," the dark entity whispers.

Although the voice resonates directly next to my left ear, I refrain from turning to look. At that moment, I became aware that the figure I thought to be my friend will not liberate me without a price. Trying to soothe my racing heart, I close my eyes and send a gulp of air down my throat, but there is no escape from this inferno. I am trapped in the being's duplicitous web with no way to alter my course without consequence. As I close my eyes tighter, a tear escapes through the slit between my lids and rolls down the bone of my cheek.

Apprehensively I reopen them and shift my eyes to my motionless right arm. I tremble as I spot the single leg of a hair-laden black spider creep from underneath my starched cuff. The light scurrying brush against my skin makes my upper body shudder. One by one, each remaining leg joins the others, and the ferocious beast exits onto the top of my glove. Its body nearly occupies the entire back of my hand, from my wrist to my knuckles. Fixated on the arachnid's movements on the navy material, I recognize the distinct red marking on its back and cringe in horror. I've been courting disaster and must alter the trajectory of my approach. It's clear the figure can see through my lies and is aware of my change of heart.

"What do you want me to do?" I ask, trying to steady my hand.

My voice wavers as it exits the back of my throat, and the shadow's laugh echoes my fear.

"Don't be frightened. It won't hurt you," the voice playfully states.

Refraining from using my hand with the spider on top of it while I talk, I keep my upper body still and inhale deeply before repeating my question.

"What do you want me to do?"

Out of my peripheral vision, I see a deep indentation form on top of the seat in front of me, followed by a harsh squeak and creak.

"You already know the answer," the voice confidently states.

I sense the shadow leaning forward and witness the seat's depression shift closer to the edge. In an attempt to move farther away, I push my back against the wall behind me.

With nowhere left to go, my body stays stationary. Helplessly I watch as each tiny icicle forms from the condensation of the figure's breath, which is inches from my face and floats to my lap. As the mysterious being closes the distance between us, I know I must change my approach in order to survive. As I stare at the bodyless figure, I pretend to see the creature's outline and find each corner of its eyes. To conceal the fear building inside me, I use all my energy to refrain from blinking. the

The mysterious friend's deep voice boils with rage: "Kill, kill, kill, kill."

Like a haunting siren's call, the sound of its voice penetrates my left eardrum, and before I have time to react, the beckoning command expels through my right ear. Rapidly I scan my thoughts to determine my subsequent actions. I believe all perpetrators remain innocent until proven guilty. Playing up my naivete regarding the situation seems like the best option for prolonging my inevitable fate. I hesitate for a moment before issuing a reply.

"My old friend, I am indebted to you. Just tell me who, and I shall do your bidding," I finally say.

My acquaintance—yes, that is how I shall refer to the being behind its back from here on—is trying to back me into a corner, and I feel like a trapped animal ready to bite. Each of the words I allow to depart from between my teeth is an unadulterated lie. No matter what I am about to face, I must remain still as my body coils like a snake waiting to strike. The air currents inside the cabin build turbulently, creating a tornado at my brow, the momentum causing the passenger-side window to open. I'm confident the sick tormentor eavesdrops on my thoughts, evidenced by the surrounding elements' transition to chaos.

As the outside elements disrupt the once-peaceful air, each of the spider's legs tries to cling to the material of my glove.

"We are both pawns in a grand scheme," I sympathize with it.

Everything continues to chaotically spiral around us. Strong currents of dark ash enter through the windows to contaminate the air. As I accidentally suck in a gulp of soot, my lungs contract, and I cough. My hands spring up from my lap to clutch the skin around my neck. The harsh movement forces the necklace to fall onto the seat beside me. Layers of ash cover the inside of the surrounding upholstery, and I jump at the sound of the window angrily slamming shut.

My acquaintance continues to fluster with rage. "Him!" the voice orders.

The command sends my heart plummeting to the pit of my stomach. Not wishing to draw unnecessary attention to my travel companion, I focus on keeping myself safe by staring forward. The uncertainty surrounding his reaction to the circumstance eats at my soul, and my eyes shift as the black widow's legs move across the seat. Each swift movement tells me it has a plan to fulfill.

Disparaging cackles rumble the carriage's walls and rattle the wheels against each spoke. Even though I'm petrified of what I might see, I reluctantly shift my attention toward the man sitting next to me. The first thing I notice is David's positioning; he is no longer staring out the window. Instead, his body sits stiffly upright, like someone has mummified him with his eyes plastered open. He eerily stares toward the shadowy figure without blinking, and I immediately recognize something is wrong.

As his lips part to speak, only a puff of ash expels from his lungs. Leaning toward him, I detect something stirring inside the back of his throat. The image consumes me with interminable dread. Like a mass exodus, a trove of tiny spiders flees to his tongue from his esophagus, the flux of rapid movement making his mouth dance like a puppet. I shift my hand toward him to wipe away a tiny discolored tear forming at the corner of his eye. Just as I'm about to touch the speck, it becomes more significant, and the unknown prompts my hand to retract to my side. Desperate to escape the horrifying scene, I push my body back, retreating into my corner of safety. The fleshy black widow that was once perched on my glove lets out a screech as it moves up David's hand resting on the seat, and I gasp at the drastic difference from the memory of him gallantly offering his palm to me earlier in the day. The unfolding scene sends convulsive cold shivers down my spine.

No is the only term I can muster in my anguished skull.

As the word resonates through my mind, the scene reveals more intricacies. What I thought to be a growing dark tear at the corner of David's eye erupts, one leg at a time, pulling its body out from the tear duct, revealing itself. Once free from the small pocket of skin, the spider's body expands. Like flooding water, a pandemonium of newborn spiders streams from every orifice of his body. His mouth opens unnaturally wide, forcing his jaw to unhinge from the socket and allowing the masses of crawling creatures a seamless exit as they spill from his lips. While the group moves in a fury of chaos, each makes poisonous bite marks under their tiny tapping feet. The scene increasingly becomes more gruesome as the crawling black flood pours from the canals of each of his innocent ears. The image is so shocking that I cannot look away.

At first glance, all the bites look like irritated hives; then, after mere seconds, they take on the essence of the venom's acidic qualities, and the toxin's virulence consumes his bare skin. Each deep crater of his disintegrative flesh becomes surrounded by boiling pustules, and the gaping sores expose his festering bones. Within a matter of moments, David's attractive features are unrecognizable under the acid-induced necrosis. Continuing their exit in abundance, the spiders cover his entire body and slowly devour him. I stare in horror as he convulses from the overload of venom. The psychological trauma created by the imagery triggers my mental collapse, and I snap without warning.

"Stop it!" I scream.

Following the scent of melting flesh engulfing the carriage, the blanket of bloodthirsty spiders fully encompasses his head, leaving not a signal recognizable feature of his once-perfect profile. The combination of the gruesome scene and putrid aroma makes my head feel faint, and I lose control.

"I swear I will do what you ask," I plead.

Two loud finger snaps echo near me. Hearing the boisterous digit's percussion next to my ear stirs my groggy mind, and the unbearable noise disorients me as I'm transported back to reality.

"Hope, wake up. Here we are," David says, waving a hand in front of my face.

The spider bites are no longer present, and the empty seat across the way is staring back at me. Looking around, I notice I fell asleep on his lap, and my face grows red with embarrassment. Quickly I push myself away from him and sit upright.

"Do you always fall asleep without warning?" he asks with a laugh.

The dream felt oddly real. As much as I try, I'm having trouble shaking my trauma from seeing the arachnids eat his flesh. The horrific smell of burned skin still lingering in my nostrils, I use my hand to fan fresh air into my face to rid myself of the smell.

"Would you mind opening a window?" I ask.

Smirking, David cracks open the window next to him. After I experienced the omen-like dream, his pleasant demeanor overwhelms me with guilt. Hiding my despair and insecurities, I nervously smile back at him, wondering what is wrong with me. Usually I would be more than willing to kill at my shadow acquaintance's whim, but something feels different. Let me rephrase my realization: it isn't something that feels different; *I* felt different.

The sound of David closing the window breaks my train of thought, and his concerned face turns to mine. "Do you feel better?"

Finally looking him directly in the eye, I manage a nod.

"Indeed," I reply.

When I turn to watch the shifting scenery outside, the distraction makes my eyes widen. The approaching estate is surprisingly massive. Towering pillars hold up a vast balcony, and each mighty cylinder-shaped block of marble appears to have been taken from the Roman Colosseum. Perfectly placed between two of the prominent pillars is the front door. I've never encountered an entrance so grand. It looks as if the door was constructed for a giant, with the double-entry nearly three times my height. As our carriage enters the roundabout made from intricately speckled stones, I have a front-row view of the ornate granite fountain. An angel spews water out of a trumpeting horn in the sculpture's center.

Briefly closing my eyes, I find the muted sound of the running water extraordinarily therapeutic and calming to my nerves. A small garden built into a maze surrounds the fountain, with each planted flowerbed sprouting colorful rosebushes to accent the estate's sophistication. Rather than the other cold, emotionless houses I've experienced, this one mimics the home of a fairy-tale prince. Turning my face, I look at David as he admires his estate from his window.

What's the catch? There must be something wrong with him.

My impression regarding his outward form, personality, and wealth confuses me. He's the perfect gentleman on paper, so why is he not married? He could have any woman of his choosing. There must be some reason the bloke is still living the single life. Maybe I'm not seeing something or he has a hidden secret. There could very well be more to him than meets the eye.

As he turns to look at me, his lips break into a smile, showing his dimples.

"What do you think of it?" he says proudly.

Taking a moment, I overthink my response and can't help wonder if what he's asking is meant as a trick question. As you know, everyone has recently revealed themselves to me as unreliable, so naturally I'm wary he may follow suit. Even though I worry, I still feel the weird gravitating pull of my soul to his exuberant smile and soft voice. He makes me want to be a better version of myself, and at this moment, I must be calm and lead with honesty for once in my life. I have to remind myself that he's different.

I clear my throat and speak. "Exquisite."

The compliment makes his face light up from ear to ear. Honestly, considering I just met the fellow, I'm unsure if my opinion will mean much to a man of such distinction, but his reaction proves differently. I smile at the thought of someone potentially admiring me for my genuine self—including my intellect. This chance meeting has opened my eyes to a world of possibilities, and I know that to live a life I previously could only dream of, I must denounce the shadow's cruel depiction of happiness from now on.

Good riddance, ol' foe. I close my eyes and...

As I reopen them to the world, I feel the sensation of being reborn as I grin at David.

"Welcome to your new home," he says, smiling.

Chapter Ten

FROLICKING WITH THE DEVIL

Exiting the carriage feels all too natural as each sole of my boot touches the cobblestones. A grounded state of mind replaces all my anxiety, and I feel as though my feet are gliding. Focusing on the beauty of the landscaping around me, I try not to fixate on the past and the mentally taxing experience the shadow forced me to endure during the lengthy travel here. More than anything, I want to escape the conflict the mysterious being conjured in an attempt to break me psychologically. Starting this new journey makes me hopeful that finally, I might be able to leave each of my false identities and experiences behind once and for all. The sound of the carriage door shutting behind me commences my life's new fresh start. No one, not even the dark figure, can stop me.

For the first time in my life, an honest-to-God possibility of discovering unadulterated happiness lies at my feet, and this euphoria is the only thing I wish to chase. After getting a small taste of the sensation, I yearn for more like a fiend for opioids. As the warming hold over my heart becomes irreplaceable, I shift the need to grasp the intoxicating emotion to the top of my list of priorities. Nothing is more necessary for my life than reliving this elation day in and day out.

The therapeutic sound of the trickling water redirects my thoughts, stopping my mind from touching on any topics regarding plans for revenge against the ominous shadow. Even though I know to remain alive I must prove my dominance over the bullying mastermind who orchestrated each of my nightmares, for now I wish to live within my pure feelings of happiness. Some may believe this is a method of avoidance; contradicting them, I consider it a way of remaining sane. As I redirect my thoughts again, I turn to admire the angel atop the fountain. The sight of the stream spitting from the angelic brass instrument compels my lips to break into a smile, and I move toward the intricate sculpture to get a better gander. Filled with curiosity, I feel David smile at me as I make my trek forward. Cooling bursts from the breeze caress each horse's conditioned mane, and petting their shining coats sparks them to whinny. My feet spin in a circle to their gleeful pleas as though I'm waltzing, and in the distance, David chuckles.

"You go ahead and explore, Hope. I'll catch up with you as soon as I finish directing Fredrick regarding where to put your luggage," he shouts with excitement.

As he points to the driver and instructs him to take care while unloading my chest, I acknowledge his words by lifting my hand above my head. Continuing my mission to find the bubbling reservoir, I maneuver around each corner of the flower-covered maze as though it's a treasure hunt.

At the beginning of the obstacle, each of the walls made of flower-laden hedges is relatively short, just reaching my kneecap. Like a trick of the mind, however, they grow taller as I move closer to the center of the circular maze.

Choosing which way to turn probably seems uneventful to most, but the element of surprise makes me ecstatic. For the first time in my life, I experience the innocence of childlike joy. Since my upbringing never condoned such behavior, the simplistic discharge of ambitions feels freeing, and it surprises me such a small thing can trigger such a pleasant response. After making a few wrong turns, I stop to listen for the noise of the running water to escalate and redirect my path to the center of the maze.

My enthusiasm for completing the maze is unmatched. As I make my last turn, I see the enchanting statuary nearing, and my eyes are ready to collect their prize. Engulfed by my surroundings, I analyze this newly discovered unfamiliar terrain and the hedges that make up the shoulder-high walls of the winner's circle. Providing a sense of privacy, the foliage barriers close off the viewing experience of the artwork from the rest of the world and offer a utopian quality. I find the maze's center to be a rewarding atmosphere that encompasses both seclusion and intimacy.

The circling hedge promotes serenity by dampening the noise from the world outside. Looking around the circle, I spot four evenly spaced concrete benches, each perfectly positioned as though idolizing the fountain's charm, with perfectly trimmed blades of grass surrounding their decorative legs. The iridescent sound of chirping lightens the still air, and as I move closer, I witness a grouping of small birds taking their morning bath. Admiring their blithe, I observe each wing splash through the flowing water, the spectacle bringing an essence of warmth to my heart. The spouting waterfall above trickles to its destination in the lower basin, promoting playful bubbles to form.

Enjoying the turbulence bestowed from above, the birds use the rippling water to wash beneath each feather. The excitement emanating from their joyous chirps uplifts my spirit. As they continue to bathe their cares away, the fresh morning sun projects rays of light upon the unique patterns of their quills and illuminates each radiant color. The array of differentiating hues resembles a new rainbow after a light rainfall. Wanting to join in, I dip my finger into the inviting water and splash along with my new friends. As they sing me a song with chirping scales, I lower myself to eye level with their playful beaks. Wanting to confide in their lovely company, I open my mouth to smile and speak.

"I'll let you in on a secret: I want nothing more than to live like you," I whisper, then whistle a chirp.

The birds happily reply by performing somersaults in the pool's water, and I smile. As I stand to my feet, I use the tips of my fingers to traipse the thick edge of the bowl's basin and shift my concentration to the highest tier of the water. My eyes follow the stream's trail to gaze at the angel playing trumpet toward the cottony clouds in the sky. Each of the progressive elements depicting the face of the sculpture reminds me of the youth of a newborn babe. Earlier in my life, I wasn't keen on the idea of birthing offspring. I could never wrap my mind around the concept of adding another helpless life to a world of corruption and hatred, but when I laid eyes on the valiant stranger, my viewpoint shifted. If I am to live my expected life of never-ending happiness with David, the idea of adding a child into the equation no longer appears to be a foreign concept to my skull. Allowing the blindsiding epiphany to infiltrate my thoughts forces a loud breath to leave my lungs, and I know only time is the deciding factor regarding our intertwining fates.

Assessing the rest of the statue's intricacies, I discern two bare concrete feet in the crystal-clear liquid, as well as effortlessly flowing clothing layering the small body like a toga. The child's hands are raised, positioned themselves on the trumpet. One set of fingers pushes down a configuration of round keys while the other grips the instrument near the mouthpiece for stability. Blowing a sizable gust of air, each cheek puffs as if to play a strenuous note to the heavens.

The innocence behind the artist's portrayal of this excellent being is immaculate, and I appreciate the nondiscriminatory choice of eliminating the sexual designation of the child. Instead, the features reflect something neutral of gender. I don't understand the concept of deeming a celestial being with one sexual identity. The idea only gives those still saddled to earth another reason to view their born predicament as superior to another.

As my eyes close, I imagine the statue in a full-color scheme with rosy cheeks and soft skin. I add life to the creature's short curly hair by lightening the rough textures with blond tones. Compared to prior times, I find exploring my thoughts a lovely experience, and the positive difference makes my life's rebirth seem possible. Tilting my head to the sky, I allow the sun's vibrant rays to dance across my skin and the warmth to thaw my damaged heart. Just as I embrace this glorious turn of events, a jabbing sensation plagues the delicate skin between my clavicle bones. The uncomfortableness contradicts all my previous notions of happiness and steals from me the stability of my experience.

It is painful, with a quick onset, equivalent to touching a hot teakettle or being branded like a rancher's cattle. Confused by the escalating agony, I lift my hands to find the source. While my hands frantically fumble for the cause, my fingertips burn as they graze the metal of the locket around my neck. I've heard of metal jewelry heating from extensive exposure to the sun, but this is different, and the sensation is unbearable. As I try to ignore the pain resonating from my charred digits, I paw for the clasp to end my misery and give my flesh a break. Stuck, I panic; no matter the extent of my effort to free myself, the piece will not budge. The awareness of my skin helplessly burning is horrifying, and the more I focus on my suffering, the worse it becomes.

Knowing what I must do, I inhale a massive breath of air, preparing for the excruciating scorch I'm about to endure. While I hold my breath, I tightly wrap my right hand around the heart-shaped locket. To offset the misery of my skin frying and refrain from screaming, I place my left hand in my mouth and bite down on it. Pulling the heart with all my might, I feel the chain breaking away from my neck and chuck the jewelry into the fountain. The water sizzles as the alloy trinket contacts the fluid. Before the locket sinks, the differentiating density prompts the surrounding water to splash before it descends to the bottom, inciting the once-exuberant birds to flee. I wave my hand in the air like a madwoman as I try to cool my scorching skin, then release my teeth from my hand.

With haste, I analyze the damage I've done to my right palm. The sight of my blistered skin makes my jaw clench as the excruciating pain lingers. A closer look reveals that the locket's engraving has transferred to my flesh, etched into my palm.

Squinting, I whisper the words. "*Quidquid voverat atque promiserat.*"

Typically, if the signature of a contract occurs under duress, the Latin phrase for "null and void" applies to the agreement. I can thank my chronic studying for making me privy to the origin and find my knowledge prompting me to question the context of the phrase in terms of my situation.

Is this my sign that the phantom figure is releasing me? Still pondering, I hold my hand closer, peering at the compilation of carvings.

The idea of having a clean break from our treacherous relationship numbs my welts and makes my heart race. All at once, I hear a tiny splash, and my head snaps away from my hand to inspect. My eyes fixed on the object. I could not decipher the identity of the little dark ball suspended in the water and take a step closer to examine it. As my foot plants to the ground, I spy a small beak in the middle of a few jostled feathers, and I recognize the corpse as one bird from the splashing group. The once-happy memory now sickens my stomach.

"You poor creature," I whisper, using my uninjured hand to scoop up the floating body. As I raise the small lifeless body to my eyes to examine it, another coinciding splash ensues. One by one, the rest of the flock falls from the sky, and their spiritless bodies float in the serene bubbling water before me. Staring at the murder scene, I stand in disbelief that they no longer produce songs of joy. After fishing each limp corpse from the water, I gently set them on the ground to dry. As I've never been in a similar situation before, I don't know what else to do.

Even though the feathered creatures are unable to move, I hope the sun will revive all their tiny hearts and force breath into their lungs. As I wait for any sign they'll return to life, I lower myself to my knees and sing a soft lullaby to comfort them.

"Come little ones, don't be afraid, for I have prayed, and you shall soon be saved. I will sweetly sing towards the devil to scare him away from our chipper day so we can resume our joyous play." I sing in a soothing melodic tone.

Each of their beady, lifeless black eyes leers at me for help. Fighting back the tears of guilt, I redirect my attention to the fountain. Taking a deep breath, I sniffle.

"I'd better check to make sure I got everyone," I quietly state to distract myself.

Rising to my feet, I rush to look for any stragglers. As I glance over the basin's edge into the clear water, I'm met with shards of light reflecting from the sunken locket. It glistens like a mesmerizing spectacle, and I can't look away. Drawn to its luster, I tilt closer to admire the metal. That's when I realize someone has tampered with its position; the locket lies open, its contents ransacked. The sight prompts my heart to stop and my mind to fill with many questions.

Is this a sick joke? Were the toxic poppy seeds the cause of the sweet flock's demise? I frantically pine.

If my unsuspecting hand caused the innocent creatures' loss of life, I can't live another day knowing I'm the source. Forever I will denounce myself as a monstrous force that gives all I touch lousy luck. With the dark wraith following my every move, no one would remain safe around me. I'm lost in my dramatic spiral, depressive sentiment clouding my judgment, and I'm once again trapped with no way of escape. Playing off my consternation, the sky above summons black storm clouds to replace the picturesque blue skyline. As sounds of lightning signal the oncoming torrential downpour, my upper body leans over the fountain bowl to look at my reflection. I need to survey who I've become and hunt for any evil in my eyes.

The image I find staring back isn't of any familiarity to me, and the sight of my deep-set sockets with dark circles makes me cringe. Once filled with life, my gaze now resembles black pools of death, and I don't know how to restore it. Although it's been apparent for some time that the murky entity killed a piece of me to inhabit, I complacently have chosen to ignore it. Feeling a delayed mourning sweep over my body, I allow myself to grieve and let the tears roll from my eyes. As each falling droplet joins the pool, the reflection staring back at me distorts, the thunder growing more robust in the purple and black sky. As I remained cowered over the base of the fountain, a flash of lightning struck over my head.

Bursts of light brush the angel's stone skull, bringing life to the stiff creation. Little by little, the child's body moves each joint and unhinges the cemented trumpet from its lips. Wiggling its fingers, it takes a deep, inhaling breath through its nose and smiles at the black clouds to give thanks. The unnaturally large smile contradicts the cherub's sculpted vibrancy. Making the holy depiction no longer anything of ideology, each corner of its mouth curls to touch the bottom of each eye, and its eerie smile embodies something from hell. The child keeps the demonic grin across its face, its stiff movements remaining disjointed from one another.

My pitiful weeping seems to bring the creature joy, and the sight of the dead birds induces the animated stone to extend its tongue to lick its top lip. Everyone's pain serves the fiend a warming sensation of pleasure. Releasing a garbled murmur, it lowers its head to look at my hunching vertebrae. As the being fixates its visual curiosity on my helpless body, it lifts its heels to tiptoe across the top water basin. After reaching the reservoir's edge with its naked toe, it lowers itself to its belly and lies still, the trumpet fixed to one hand. Leaning over the edge, it silently watches from above.

While my woes fester, I embrace the coldness of the increasing rainfall that pummels the back of my neck and back—just as I felt deserving of hypothermia earlier in the carriage. Hearing a deep cackle above me, I tilt my gaze up and am met with the angel's stone-cold demonic stare and the oblong smile still plastered on its face. Before I can stand to defend myself, it swims toward me like a serpent and seizes a handful of my hair. Its stony clutch on my locks sends my body into a fit of shock, and its violent jerking releases a loud snap from my neck. Cackling at my plea for help, the entity dunks my head into the chilled basin of water.

My legs kick and my arms flail as I try to breathe. Trying to inhale a gulp of air, my lungs fill with more water and I panic. I'm drowning and no one is around to rescue me. Each time I think my life is over, the monstrosity lifts my head into the chilly air to tease me before thrusting my head back into the bowl. Unable to fight the force any longer, my body loses hope. The relief I feel knowing my demise is fast approaching will forever be a moment I'll never forget. If I die, I can never hurt David, and he'll live a normal life. Just as I'm at peace with my predicament, the beast pulls me to the surface and takes one last look into my eyes. Its intentions are obvious: it only desires to feast off my suffering.

Though the being's eyes were crafted from stone, it's still apparent that there's no soul behind their lifeless vision, and immediately I recognized my battle with the shadow is not over. If I don't perform its sadistic bidding, it will never allow me the freedom to live a life of normalcy and peace. Based on the shadow's cruel treatment, it's evident that killing me isn't part of its plan, because that would end my suffering. Instead of wishing me dead, it wants to condemn me to a life crafted by fear. I hear a distant hedge rustle and the fiend turns its head to look.

"Hope?" David calls.

The being lets out a shriek that sounds like the roar of a lioness, then cranks its head back to look into my eyes. As it opens its mouth, I smell rotting flesh.

"Looks like it's a soiree," the monster says with a demonic laugh.

Not if I can help it, I think, clenching my fists.

Unable to move my head, I strain to look toward David's traveling voice. After coughing up the remaining water from my lungs, I answer him. "I'm just enjoying the marvelous fountain!" I call out, trembling from the trauma.

As I worry my tone might give away my body's distress, adrenaline fills my heart.

"You think you can be happy with that pompous fool?" the living statue states. "He will tire of you and throw you to the street as though you're a plagued piece of trash. Just wait; he will see through your facade."

Closing my eyes, I ignore the monster and listen for David's footsteps, which are quickly approaching.

"You're wrong," I reply, and spit in its face.

"I promise I will be right there! I haven't had to find my way through this maze in ages, so I'm a little rusty," David says with an awkward laugh to cover his embarrassment.

The creature holding me hostage tightens its grip around my hair and lengthens its grin. "Shall I wait and finish your torture in front of the knight who meanders to save you?" it says.

As I open my eyes to stare into its soul, rage fills my limbs and my boiling blood brings me joy, prompting me to challenge the demented being. "Kill me now," I state.

In disbelief, I watch as my words fuel its contorting face. Its smile grows even more significant than it would in life, and the lengthening nature of its lips causes cracks to splice the lids of each eye. Seizing the moment, I raise my hands and place a finger in each eye socket. Each of my digits presses as hard as it can to blind the creature. As the beast drops me to the ground, I gasp to catch my breath. Looking up to see the being's next move, I discover the clearing sky and the statue's return to its normal state. Even though the shadow has already retreated, I'm still stuck in fight-or-flight mode, my heart pounding in my chest. The sound of happy chirps prompts me to scan the surrounding grounds, but when I look around, I see all the birds have vanished.

"You have endured much worse—you'll be fine," I mutter to myself, picking myself up from the ground and brushing the remnants of freshly cut grass off my dress.

Looking around the utopia, I rush to one of the benches to take a seat and set the scene. If I am to be granted an everyday life, I must look calm and collected. As I adjust my position, I notice the locket is still around my neck; I tighten my jaw as a shiver rolls down my spine. As laughter resonates from the direction of the statue, my head snaps up to look, but there is no sign that the carved creature has regained life. Trying to stay strong, I take a deep breath to calm my paranoia.

Am I going crazy? My racing thoughts make me feel alone.

The nearby hedge rustles louder, and a hand appears. Grasping the corner of the flowering hedge, David springs around to reveal himself. "Found you!" he says, smiling.

Placing the series of happenings in the past, I hysterically giggle at him, and he joins in on the laughter.

"I dare say I've never been happier to see another individual in my life," I state.

My words prompt him to sprint toward me, then reach for my hand to help pull me up. As I extend my hand toward him, I notice a few minor scratches where the scorching locket etched words into my skin.

David looks concerned as he follows my gaze, then flips my hand over to inspect. "I can't leave you alone for mere seconds without you getting hurt," he says, smirking flirtatiously.

As I retract my hand, memories from my painful encounter with the locket race through my mind. I find it increasingly difficult to see where reality starts and my imagination ends. The shadow left the brand as a warning, and I can't help wonder what else the being may be capable of.

"Clumsy me. I must have caught myself on one of the rosebushes." I shrug then hold my palm to his cheek.

He takes my hand. "Well then, shall we head inside to start your tour?" he asks, his eyes shining with excitement.

Taking a quick look back at the statue, I grab his hand tighter and grin. "Yes. I think I've had enough fresh air for a lifetime."

He scrutinizes the statue and offers me a smile. "So similar to my ward. The artist modeled the angel's likeness on my sweet nephew."

"Isn't that something?" I say with a nervous laugh, keeping my eyes forward.

Of course, it's a male, I think, rolling my eyes.

Hoping I never have to meet the statue's counterpart, I gaze at the estate. As David's grip on my hand tightens, we look each other in the eye and all my worldly problems disappear. Then, as we exit the maze of terror, I catch a sudden laugh behind me.

"Just wait," the mysterious voice whispers from the fountain.

Chapter Eleven

THE LETTER M

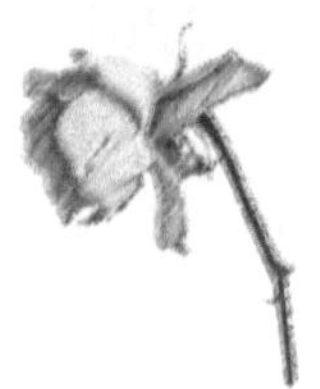

Typically, a tour of someone's estate is relatively short, but with David's behavior and enthusiasm far from ordinary, this tour was different. Much of our time has been spent discovering new sights between the great walls. When I first stepped through the enormous front doors, my lips grew dry, and words shriveled on my tongue like sponges left in the sun. My speech remains lost in my mouth; I focus on taking advantage of my other senses and silently observing my surroundings.

As I'm swept away by my sensory experiences, I know the glorious appearance of the entryway meets every one of my expectations. Each extravagant detail reveals that everything has been selected by hand, and the decorator's taste was of the utmost influence. I find all the decor exquisite to the eye as the two carved front doors, and all the signs of affluence meet my strict requirements for a permanent home.

David's dress shoes click against the marble floor as I follow him through the long front room. As we walk, my eyes are drawn to the intricacies of the vaulted ceiling, but an exciting display of beauty pleasantly pulls away my focus. Above my head hangs a mural of jubilant angels flying to the silent tune of exalting hymns. The scene weaves between the sturdy wooden pillars that support the walls. I swear each of the cherubic beings has a glowing smile hiding behind the pupils of their dreamy eyes and looks happier than the next. Fixated on the innocence of their flying bodies, I see their movement come to life before my eyes, and I intently observe them with my inquisitive stare.

What is this man's fascination with angels and baby ones at that?

Living up to the angelic stereotype I saw fashioned by the statue in the fountain, they drape all their tiny bodies with flowing loincloths, and some carry brass instruments amid the translucent clouds. The army of little creatures makes my nerves spiral out of control. The vast similarities between them and the angel at the fountain trigger a response through every inch of my body, causing terminal shudders to dance down my bones from repressed fright.

Noticing my focus, David's eyes follow my gaze to the mural and he smiles. As he inhales a deep breath, his excitement grows. "Happy to see you're taken with the angel theme," he says, his right hand gliding toward the flying forms cascading above our heads.

Wanting to act respectfully, I clear my throat to cover up my disdain and purse my lips to speak. "Yes, they are very inspirational. I find their small bodies grant permission to a plethora of my keen thoughts," I say, my knees locking under my dress in an attempt to stop the waves of shaking.

My words cause his mannerisms to ramp up with excitement. As I remain at a standstill, contemplating his joy, I sense something obscure creeping near the edge of my line of sight and freeze my stare in David's direction. Getting another glimpse of one of the little creature's toes wiggling in my peripheral view validates my fears and summons my head to look. If I am to show others my haunting, I will have to catch it in the act, but before my vision can entirely focus, David's mouth opens to chime in. His gasp expels a higher level of excitement into the air and contradicts my internalized terror.

"I too, find the sight of each of their innocent bodies sprinkling the entire manor inspirational. You shall be excited to know there is quite the extravagant angelic display in your quarters; it's like they all flew into your room to greet you," he proudly states, his hands flying through the air to simulate a fairy-like glide.

Instead of brightening my spirits, his magical theatrics feed my imaginings of the creatures coming to life and triggers a response from my nervous system. My overwhelming fright makes me gasp as my eyes follow the trail of flying children dancing into the far distance. Trying to cover my paling appearance, I force myself to match David's smile and the excitement in his eyes. He cannot know the truth behind the powerful feelings building inside me.

"What a joy their company will be to my waking eyes," I say through my teeth, housing a clenched grin.

He's barely buying my fraudulent enthusiasm.

I find the presence of their tiny ears intently listening to my words and their eyes critiquing each of my charades unsettling. One by one, all the unwelcome stares judge my body's movements, and a suffocating sensation wraps around the top of my ribs. Their obnoxious infestation is like a flock of pesky mosquitoes buzzing around my ears. As the angels continue to watch my every move, an eerie gray fog sweeps through my mind. By the mocking tone of the trolling devil, it is evident this is yet another cruel joke being projected by the sickening shadowy figure.

As my thoughts regarding the mysterious being's childish ways conclude, a nondescript laugh sounds from the far corner of the room and confirms my suspicion. Trying not to give my spiteful acquaintance any indication of satisfaction or credit, I slowly pivot my body to redirect my attention to the man of honor who is lovestruck and ogling my face to admire my beauty. His eyes are like small puppies, patiently waiting for any sign of emotional reciprocation. The sigh triggers guilt to plague my scattering thoughts and sorrow to fill the pit of my stomach. I want nothing more than a moment alone to contemplate my observations. I know I must escape the lovely company of David to recoup my plan for defense against my enemy. To evoke genuine sympathy, he must pity me for my suffering. Releasing a quick yawn, I attempt to act fragile and physically worn.

"Speaking of those precious heaven-sent angels, if you don't mind excusing me, I would love to be shown to my room so I can freshen up from my travels," I say with an essence of a warming smile.

David's fingers nervously fidget by his sides. My words cause the poor man to worry and his once-enthusiastic mannerisms to scramble. He flounders to scrap up an apology for not offering the necessity sooner.

"Of course. Yes, yes, where are my manners? My sincerest apologies. You must be exhausted," he says, lifting his fingers and snapping them.

The harsh clicking reverberates throughout the otherwise-peaceful environment, making me wince. Still on edge, I jump at the echo of soft footsteps approaching from behind me. Although my mind reels with spiraling ideas regarding the figure's identity behind the march, I refrain from looking. As David summons the figure closer, the mystery continues to wreck my mind, and while I stew in my anxiety, the pace of the footfalls quickens.

David throws his hands up into the air with an open-mouth smile. "Aha, there she is!"

Drawing attention to her, he uses the swing of his hands to point to her in a showcasing manner, and I'm surprised by my eyes' discovery. A small-statured woman stands before us wearing a modest navy-blue dress, hair in a white lace bonnet and an apron to match tied around her waist. She avoids eye contact with me by diverting her eyes to the floor tiles. Even though she appears fit, her slight wrinkles reveal she is nearly a decade older than David. Her mannerisms exude anxiety, and the fact that she won't look at me makes me wary of her character.

Putting on a fake smile to warm my appearance, I stare in her direction while enthusiastically addressing David. "You must tell me about this lovely creature joining us," I offer.

Although I direct my inquisitive statement to my host, I use over-accentuated diction to entice her. As I finish speaking, I try with all my energy to lure her gaze, even adding slight bobs of my head, which makes me look like a cobra dancing to a charmer's song. I must admit the girl's reflexes are quick; when she successfully dodges my stare like I'm the bubonic plague, I can't help find her evading skills impressive. David's oblivion to the awkwardness of the building tension comes as no shock. Blissfully he smiles at our interaction and answers me, joining the conversation.

Taking a scant breath, he continues with her lengthy introduction.

"Yes, splendid. Hope, this is Elizabeth. She will show you to your room. During your time here, she will be at your beck and call for all your needs," he states, then summons her to take a step closer.

So she's merely another chambermaid, I think, summarizing his explanation.

At last Elizabeth achieves eye contact with me, and I grin in acquiescence with my previous thought.

"Indeed," I say, bowing my head to greet her.

Our warm interaction makes David grin from ear to ear. "Very good then! I'll give you two some privacy and wait in my study for your return," he says with a twinkling eye.

I nod at his words, and he extends his hand to take hold of mine. After delicately taking my fingers, he lightly kisses the back of my palm and grins. Leaving him standing in place, we walk away. When I turn back to take one last glance in his direction, his face embraces a shade of strawberry pink. His blushing cheeks brighten as my hand rises to my shoulder to wave, and he flirtatiously lifts his hand to signal back at me. My coquettish mood abruptly shifts as my eyes catch sight of something scurrying across the base of his elevated palm, then crawling under his cuff and disappearing. The presence of the giant black arachnid wipes the smile off my face and sends a jarring tremble down my spine.

David senses my mood's shifting temperature. Frantically his eyes follow my stare down to the sleeve of his coat, scanning for the culprit behind my wavering emotions. The desperation of his action triggers a deep cackle from the room's corner and emphasizes the shadow's growing jealousy. I find the attempt at sabotaging my relationship less subtle than before, and the unknown magnitude of the shadow's vengeance drenches my soul in terror.

Lifting my fingers to my lips, I stand my ground by forming a puckering expression and blowing David a kiss. As he gazes up to see my blatant coquetting, my action shifts his underlying worries to adoration. Diverting the ominous beings' attempt at derailing my relationship makes me chuckle. As we exit the room toward the enormous staircase, I seize a moment when no one is looking and poke my tongue out at the dark corner. In response, the devious laughter in my ear abruptly stops, the thought of my behavior perturbing the figure bringing a smile to my face.

If a challenge is what you want, that is what you shall receive, I think, my ego feeding off the certainty of my successful intimidation.

Even if I were unsure about my exact plan of action, nothing would come between me and my quest to find irreplaceable happiness. I can stick up for my own needs and voice my opinions; I'm comfortable in my God-given skin, and for the first time, I'm able to embrace my true worth.

I would enlist anyone, even a phantom, to kill me before I ever let myself return to the same insecure shell of a woman I was before. If defeating the satanic creature means freely marrying David and having all my wishes come true, I know it's what I must do. Having dealt with much worse, I can easily survive the earthly hell by taking each day one step at a time. It's minuscule compared to the treachery I've been forced to endure, and the award waiting for me is worth every fight.

"This way, miss," Elizabeth calls, her open hand motioning for me to follow her.

I exit the foyer into the adjoining room, where an extraordinary staircase provides the chamber's grand focal point. The enormous structure takes up nearly half the room's square footage, and the elaborate architectural elements do not disappoint. The railing is ornately carved, depicting tree branches with abundant leaves. The weight of the massive staircase is supported by sizeable gold-accented carved wooden newel posts, the whimsical design giving an ambiance of grounding earth. Each step is made of sparkling speckled cream-colored marble and accented with knotless cherrywood.

As Elizabeth and I make our way up each stunning step, I think how glorious it would be if this sight became part of my daily existence. Looking over the railing, I'm drawn to a large chandelier. The familiarity engulfs my wandering eyes, reminding me of the recurring vision I have each night when my mind enters a dream state. The fixture's glass crystals are fashioned after the wood carvings in the staircase, and each of the lighting fixture's extending arms has dangling oval-shaped pieces of perfectly cut opalescent glass. The sight resembles freshly pruned trees, and the vivid remembrance makes me at ease, bringing peace over my thoughts.

Cascading up the remaining steps, we ascend to the upper floor and travel down a long hallway. Every turn we take, I relish in the magic surging through the air, reminding me that I'm home once and for all. The only way someone could compel me to leave is if they were to drag my corpse out, and I know even in death, I would kick and scream every step of the way. So you can better visualize why I'm so fervent about never wanting to leave the estate's grounds, I shall reveal more details regarding the extravagant interior.

An imported carpet runner with a royal burgundy and gold baroque pattern lines the center of the wooden hallway. As the daylight escapes from outside, I notice the hall darkening, illuminated by golden sconces lining the walls, providing us with the necessary lighting to complete our journey. Each warmly lit candle is strategically stationed next to showcase paintings that depict affluent family members. My curiosity piqued, I slow my pace to catch a glimpse of the beautifully executed oil paintings. I pause to look at the depiction of the man who stole my heart and granted me happiness. I find the realism of the portrait unbeatable, and the chambermaid detects my fascination.

"It's an excellent likeness, isn't it, miss?" Elizabeth says, walking toward me to join my assessment.

Admiring David's masculine features, I break my gaze to nod. "Yes, indeed so," I respond with a smile.

His slim-fitting tailcoat is fashionably regal, with dark-green velvet piping down each lapel, and his hair is perfectly quaffed to one side. Carried away by the picture, I fantasize about our time together so far and allow the happiness to trickle across my nerves.

The maid chimes in, serving as my honorary tour guide. "As you can see, the family frequently commissioned portraits of him during his childhood," she says, pointing to other portraits of David on the walls.

Thinking of his privileged childhood makes me chuckle. "Oh, if this is the worst thing you have to put up with as an only child, I'm sure his parents must have loved to spoil him rotten," I state, my eyes shift back to the portrait of my host.

A look of confusion floods her once-exuberant face, but before I can interpret her peculiar reaction, she opens her mouth to speak. "Only child?"

I pause and giggle to lighten her mood. Continuing, I try to explain myself. "With portraits as extravagant as these, I have no doubts regarding their elation over birthing a son," I reply.

Her eyes light up, my explanation resonating with her. "Oh, of course, miss. They were very pleased, but he wasn't the only child. There was a second boy."

I pause again to process my confusion. "Oh?" I reply, prompting her to continue.

Lifting a candle from the sconce stationed next to the portrait of David, Elizabeth uses the dim flickering light to lead our way to an older family portrait. The textured oil painting shows both proud parents sitting on carved wooden chairs with red velvet accents on each cushion. At their feet, two small boys of similar appearance are playing.

"See, these are David's mother and father, and those are the two boys," she says with a soft smile while pointing to each image.

Stepping forward to look closer I formulate a suitable comment. "There is so much likeness between the two, and they look rather close in age. I'm quite taken aback that he never mentioned a brother."

As I'm processing the new information, my words fall silent, and I wait for the maid to flood my ears with gossip.

"It was quite the scandal. They share the same father, but each has a different mother. For a time, it was all the chatter," she states, waving the candle closer so I can analyze the brushstrokes.

My eyes widen at the shocking information.

"So avant-garde," I reply, not knowing how else to respond.

Again I look at the mother and father, displaying perfect posture while perched above the children. As I analyze them, I pay close attention to their facial features and any slight genetic differences.

My curiosity regarding the peculiar situation heightens. "Where is the other boy's mother?"

I'm confident the couple's marital partnering appears quite suitable on paper. Still, the portrait reveals no romantic chemistry in their eyes, and their engagement presents as being more like that of a business transaction than a loving partnership. The father's smug look, along with his nose, which tips to the sky, makes it clear he loves himself more than others. This includes the woman positioned next to him. The man is dressed in a uniform resembling what a duke or someone else of influence might wear, with the outfits of his family members complementing it. Monogrammed onto his pocket is the cursive letter *M,* and based on his self-righteous expression, he was the one who selected the ensemble the others were forced to match.

The maid lets out an enormous sigh. "It's a sad story," she states. "She worked the streets; no one knew much about the creature aside from her disgraceful profession and seductive ways. The woman fell pregnant around the time of the happy couple's engagement. She endeavored to get him to break things off with his betrothed so they could be together—some nerve she had. When he refused, she disappeared and was never heard from again. It took a bit to find the child, and being the good Christians they were, of course, they couldn't stand letting the small babe live a life like hers, so they took him in."

Reluctantly I nod, attentively listening to each word falling from her gossiping lips. "Such a pity," I respond with hesitancy.

Motioning with the candle for me to follow her, she moves to a painting farther down the wall, and I follow closely to look.

"This is David's brother in his later years—a much better resemblance. I dare say he is quite handsome," she states, pointing to the portrait.

Out of curiosity about her high regard, I creep closer to get a better look. As I enter further into the candle's illumination, I see a portrait of a young man dressed in an all-black coat and tails and a tall hat, with a gold cane in his grip. Immediately every nerve in my body turns on edge, and the hair stands on my arms. Nausea floods my core and my skin turns clammy.

While I try to process my thoughts, a string of words spills out from my lips. "Indeed he is," I say, my voice trembling.

Feeling myself falling into a state of shock, I lift my left fingers to my right arm and pinch my skin, hoping I only need to wake from a nightmare.

It can't be.

"If you don't mind me asking, what is the fellow's name?" I inquire, not sure I want her to answer.

Elizabeth's lively mannerisms indicate she is waiting with bated breath to divulge the information about him. "I do not mind in the least. The woman of the residence fancied the idea of having the boys' names somewhat match, like their clothing, so she gave him the name Daniel," she says with a giggle.

Each of her words echoes in my ears as my eyes refuse to blink.

No. The harsh word floods my mind.

"As you can imagine, on account of them being two vastly different children, they didn't like the idea of showing any semblance of being twins," she states.

Trying to control my shaking hands, I slow my breathing to calm the waves of anxiety that attempt to drown me. Even though I prefer to run away from the situation, I clear my throat to prepare to utter further inquiries as I watch her admire the young man's portrait.

I speak slowly to cover the waver in my voice. "Where is he now?"

As she turns and faces me, I can tell the topic upsets her, and she takes a moment of pause.

"Again, quite a sad story," she begins. "Several years ago, a devastating accident, the details of which I prefer not to revisit, took their parents' lives. The morning following the tragedy, Daniel didn't arrive for breakfast as usual. When a servant checked his room, he was nowhere to be found, and a number of his personal belongings were missing. We're certain he used the family's trusted driver to run away and believe he couldn't cope with the pain of remaining here after losing the only mother he had known. Poor Daniel left a note regarding his melancholy and asked David to take care of a child he had been keeping secret from the family. Just like him, the child was born out of wedlock, and of course David accepted him as his ward."

At least there's one minor fact that's positive. The idea paints a slight grin on my lips.

"David truly is a saint," I swiftly chime in.

The maid nods and smiles as she reflects on something infiltrating her mind.

Raising a finger, I signal an idea and take advantage of her good mood. "Now that I think about it, I noticed the letter *M* embroidered on his father's coat in the family portrait earlier. What's the correlation?" I ask to confirm my suspicion.

Her face lights up as she races back to the family portrait to take a look. Following her, I catch a glimpse of the eyes shifting in each painting we pass and quicken my pace to catch up with her.

"Ah, yes. So insightful, miss. The letter *M* stands for 'Manley.' That is the family's surname," she says with a spark of excitement.

Although I already assumed the answer, I didn't want to believe it was the same man. My stomach falls ill as everything swirls around me.

"Oh, silly me. Of course," I say.

The confirmation paralyzes me as flashbacks from my first meeting with Daniel Manley ensue. His ghastly grin and stench of dead flesh fill my senses and cling to the walls of my mind as I'm forced to relive the horrific dream sequence I experience night after night.

As Elizabeth turns toward me, concern falls over her face. "Are you well? You look flushed, miss," she says, placing the candle back on the sconce to assist me.

I hold my hand straight out to signal for her to stop her worry, but the motion makes my worsening vision more evident. The stressful events of the past few days takes an emotional toll on my health, and I place the palm of my hand on my forehead to stop the room from spinning. Although everything around me contributes to my dizziness, I force a tiny smile across my lips.

"The brunt of the trip must be hitting my nerves," I say, looking up at her and chuckling.

"Of course. Let me show you to your room so you can lie down," she says, rushing to stabilize my wobbling body.

With every step, my vision becomes darker, as though I'm fumbling my way down the hall with fogged goggles over my eyes. Each shadow-laden space resting between the edges of the sconces' candlelight is daunting and accompanied by mocking laughter whose tonal quality stings my ears. I avoid eye contact with every nook and cranny leading to my quarters. Every step takes a lifetime, and the toil of my labored movement is magnified by my legs faltering beneath me. My world feels condemned to damnation as everything spirals and a plethora of questions floods my anxious mind.

Is this my punishment for falling in love with David and renouncing the shadow? Was this always the sadistic entity's plan? Thoughts swirl in my head like an egg being whisked.

"Only a few more steps, miss," Elizabeth says, gesturing to an open door in the distance.

Thank God. My sanctuary is within my reach, and it will only be mere seconds before I'm left alone to contemplate a plan.

Thrilled that a respite is a few steps away, I smile at her and pick up my pace. As I approach my room, the voices surrounding me grow louder with rambunctious chatter, taunting me with aggressive intonations.

"You have made your bed, and now you must lie in it, lie in it, lie in it," a deep voice whispers in my ear.

The ominous words make the hairs on my neck stand on edge. I cover the openings of my ears with my hands to force the echo to stop.

"We're almost there, and then you can rest before dinner," she says.

Her words cause me to become further overwhelmed as they add to the chaos, and my arms compulsively tremble. Elizabeth uses her hand to usher me to the open door. Pinching my eyes shut, I tune out the surrounding noise to gather my thoughts.

Why did she mention dinner?

"Dinner?" I ask.

As we reach the room's entry, she steps behind me and gently places her hand on my back for support.

"Yes, David will expect you in an hour for dinner. Don't worry—just rest and I'll be back to fetch you when it's time," she states, then nudges me through the door.

I nod to acknowledge her words and take in a deep gulp of air to calm my nerves. Scanning my surroundings, I realize why the room disappoints me. It is plagued with masculinity. The lack of color in the decorations takes life away from the wall's bones. Wood panels accent most of the barriers and match the flooring, making the patriarchal ambiance slightly rustic. As I resume poring over the bed chamber's aesthetics, the room continues to spin. I momentarily gain my bearings to scour for my trunk. Upon spotting it in the corner, I hasten in the bed's direction and stabilize myself against its sturdy wood-carved frame.

The sight of a dress laid across the pristinely made bed irks my core. Even though I can only see the generalized structure and coloring of the garment, I know it's the same one David's mother wore in their family photo. My knees tremble and my head grows faint. Noticing my falling body, Elizabeth rushes toward me. Her arms snatch the dress from the silk bedcover and hang it on the canopy railing.

"He gave me orders for you to wear this gown for dinner tonight. I will leave it here for safekeeping," she says as the garment sways.

My mind furiously spins as I collapse onto the bed. I hear the maid's feet shuffle from the room as she exits to allow me a moment of rest. As the door shuts, I fumble for the locket around my neck. I know the contents will work as a remedy for my nausea and frantic thoughts. After swiftly prying it open, I take out a single seed and place it in my mouth. With my flesh and bones too exhausted to contend with my horrific nightmares, taking the poppy will loosen my mind and allow my eyes to rest before dinner. As the room whirls around me, the shadow's voice trickles from the corner to mock me.

"Good night, Mrs. Manley," it says with a devilish laugh.

Even though the sound makes me want to open my eyes, it is too late; the poppy seed's sedative properties kick in, and I drift into a peaceful sleep.

Chapter Twelve

CHECKMATE

Polluting knocks on the cherrywood door thrust my eyes open. The time I was permitted to sleep seemed like mere seconds. Forcing myself to awaken, I lie on top of the covers and look up to see the dress still swaying. My thoughts turn into an eerie panic; still suffering from spinning vision, I realize the poppy seed's hallucinogenic properties have yet to wear off. The experience is uncharacteristic of me, and I squeeze the fingers on my right hand to shake off the nightmare. Nothing in my body, however, seems to be functioning, and the ordeal is similar to being entombed in stone. Although I know the root cause for my general lethargy, I still can't entirely wrap my brain around the extensive nature of my problematic, twisting fate. The knocking sounds continue to amass as the reverberations overlap, filling the chamber and escalating my frustration.

Bloody hell.

I'm met with a numbing sensation as I try to wiggle my toes inside my boots, and the forcefulness of my attempt causes tiny tingling pricks to stab the nerve endings on each fleshy pad. As I labor to sit up, my tenacious endeavor is unsuccessful, and panic ensues. It appears nothing is working, and my eyes are stuck with a limited range of motion. I'm immobile, my body stiff as a board, and it's as though both my shoulders are glued against the mattress. I can only use my functioning pupils, which scan my surroundings to identify what is fettering me to the bed.

As the gown continues to sway, a droplet of water hits the center of my forehead, and my irises shift to discover the source. I'm shocked to see a spectral figure sitting behind me near the headboard. It leans over the top of my skull to better investigate my petrified state, providing me a clear look at features that allude to perfect masculinity while the being was alive. The sight of the decaying soul prompts my eyes to widen with the fear of death, and I can't help wonder if it is planning my worldly exit.

"How do you like my quarters?" the male states, his fingers caressing a stray curl falling from my frazzled updo.

His digits are ice cold, and his flesh is prune-like against the delicate skin covering my skull. A grin stretches across his face, exposing each of his bone-white teeth, his gaped mouth allowing saliva to drip as he riotously laughs at my attempt to move my body. Another knock comes, this one louder than before. Without warning, the figure hunching over me takes on a human form, and the lacerations around his neck become more prominent in the light. Aggressively taking my head between his hands, he forcefully tilts it to behold the shadowed corner and laughs maniacally. The shriek from his ear-shattering cackle sucks the air from my lungs, and I immediately know the man's identity.

"Daniel?" I ask with a sense of surety.

He smiles at me and tilts his head to tip his hat.

"Yes, I am Daniel. Welcome to my humble estate."

The shadow expands significantly, overflowing its residence and pouring forth in our direction. Daniel's eyes gleefully fixate on the growing darkness while I focus on the rapidly approaching murky air. As it reaches his nostrils, he takes a giant whiff, filtering it into his brain.

When he finishes his inhalation, he opens his mouth to whisper. "Each night, after they tucked me in, I admired the shadow that dwells in that corner. Only from it did I discover comfort from my nightmares, both present, and past."

He pauses to run his fingers down the side of my temple. As the tip of his fingernail scratches the cartilage at the top of my ear, I try to flinch but cannot. Immense discomfort fills my body, and rage seethes through my jaw. Daniel takes a deep breath, the noise from the air entering his crushed trachea sounding raspy. His hands pin my shoulders down with more force as the darkness creeps over my feet and up my paralyzed legs.

"It will dispose of you just like it did me," he states, grinning at the shifting shadow.

From his cynical words, I know if I want to survive, I must escape. As I try to move my fingers again, I sense a change, and this time, my single thumb gives a slight wiggle. The shadow oozes up my torso, sparking a malevolent passion to flood my veins.

"It's coming," Daniel whispers next to my ear.

As the darkness engulfs my limbs, rage dances beneath my breast, and I smile at his lie.

"No," I unflinchingly state.

At my words, frustration brews in his core. Daniel stares at my eyes, lowers his lips to my skin, and lightly kisses each lid. Forcing my eyes to close tighter, I focus on convincing my fingers to move, and the invisible hold over my arms releases. As Daniel's lips remain on one of my vulnerable eyelids, my hands spring up to his vascular neck like angry snakes, and the sound of choking echoes in the room for several minutes. As his gagging finally quiets, his head collapses to the side of my grip and his body goes limp, filling my soul with joy. Curious to gaze upon his corpse, I leave my hands clutching his throat and allow my eyes to gawk at my victory.

The stench of death makes me grimace. Upon opening my eyes, I encounter his body's shifting clothing. Surprised to see more feminine attire has replaced his traditional ensemble, I continue my survey, moving my gaze to my cramping hands, which are locked tightly around his neck. Staring into the creature's lifeless irises causes a rush of terror to flood my skin. The face is distinct and the body isn't Daniel's. As my hands release the limp neck, I remain stunned as Elizabeth's body falls to the bed. With her eyes still open, she stares at me in disbelief, while the presence in the dark corner laughs deeply at my mistake.

"Monster, monster, monster," the mysterious voice chants.

Hearing the devious words accompany the sight of the maid's corpse sprawled across my bed sparks discord to deluge my flesh and bones. The accusation fills me with outrage.

"I am not," I reply.

As I peer in the voice's direction, I discern the outline of Daniel Manley deviously glaring back at me.

"You are the monster, not me!" I say, pointing at him, and my throat releases a grunt of anger.

My eyes drift up to the hanging dress and I cringe. In a flash I spring to my feet and tear it down. As I hurl it onto the bed, I let out a scream. Trying to catch my breath, I back to the corner and notice Daniel has vanished. The bedroom door creaks as it mysteriously drifts open, and my head turns to look. A man's footsteps can be heard traveling past on the other side of the unsealed entry. Turning to address the maid, I take a moment of pause, and then, seizing a quick gasp, I vomit a trail of words.

"I hope there are no ill feelings, dear. You must be quite aware I didn't mean to kill you," I state.

I'm met with silence as her wide-open eyes continue to stare at me. Out of irritation, I pace the room, running my fingers through my hair. As I turn to walk back, I throw my hands up to the ceiling and stomp my feet with annoyance. A deep chortle infiltrates my emotional tussle from across the room, its sardonic tone infuriating me.

"Go to hell!" I shout, throwing my hands at the shadowed corner.

My mind festers with what to do next, and then all at once, I remember the maid blathering about dinner with David. I tidy the ensemble still on my body from my travels, my fingers frantically working to smooth the garment's wrinkles.

Turning back to face Elizabeth, I let out a sigh to calm myself. "How do I look? Suitable for dinner with my future husband?" I ask with amusement.

Her face remains emotionless and dead. Irritation takes over my body due to her lack of words and lifeless gaze. My heartbeats escalate in frequency.

"For a woman of so many words, it is quite perplexing that you have not one to share. It is of no consequence, however; no one gives a damn about your opinion anyway," I state, my feet pivoting toward the open bedroom door.

Swiftly I exit the room and close the door behind me, refraining from looking at any of the portraits as I run to the stairwell. As I quicken my pace, I hear building steps escalating behind me and I run faster. As I reach the landing of the stairs, the texture of the solid wooden banister underneath my fingertips feels like heaven.

I pivot to guffaw at the dark hallway behind me. "Ha!" I state, just before turning and walking down the cascading steps.

As I reach the base of the staircase, a weight lifts from my shoulders, and closing my eyes, I gather my bearings. Intently I listen for clues that may lead me toward the dining room, and a moment later, my feet glide to the sound of silverware striking a wooden table. My body jars to the right and moves with haste down the hallway, in the opposite direction of the foyer. In the distance, a shining light comes from an archway. As I gaze up to the ceiling, I see the mural of cherubs flying above my head and realize they are guiding the way to David.

When I reach the golden arch, I peer inside the doorless entry and see an ornate banquet-style dining table decorated with gold-threaded linens. Several candles provide dim lighting for the dinner seating, while extravagant fruit arrangements surround each stick of illuminated wax. As David sits patiently, stationed at the farthest seat from the entry, his mere presence makes me smile. Nervously I graze the room with my stare, and the sight of two small children, one boy and one girl, sitting beside him, catches my attention. They laugh together as they await my arrival.

When I clear my throat, all three turn their heads to look at me as I enter the room. David stands and rushes to my side, greeting me enthusiastically. As he approaches, he scans behind me as if searching for something.

"That's odd. Elizabeth must have gone to do chores," he says with a shrug.

He points toward the table, extends his forearm for me to grasp, and we glide to our designated settings.

"I must apologize for not wearing the dress you chose for me," I nervously tell him.

He raises an eyebrow. "Dress?"

The image of the gown lying across my bed provides me the mental ammunition I need to validate my truth. I start my rebuttal by placing a warm smile on my face.

"Yes, you remember the beautiful velvet ensemble you told sweet Elizabeth to pull for me to wear?" I reply, my left hand fidgeting.

His eyes shift as he ponders. "I don't recall that, but I can be absentminded. My preoccupation with caring for my ward causes me to be quite forgetful sometimes. Regardless, you are ravishing in everything you wear. I dare say it is one of your most alluring qualities," he states, pulling a chair out for me to sit.

His compliments make me blush, and I look away with nervous apprehension at the archway to hide my rosy cheeks.

"You are too kind," I say with a smirk.

His chuckle emanates from behind me as he pushes in my chair, and the sound of his laughter warms my heart. Just as the last bit of anxiety exits my core, I catch a glimpse of a shadowy figure drifting past the doorway, and my body becomes rigid with tension. Taking a calming breath, I turn toward David as he makes his way to his place across from me at the long table. The children grin as he sits between them. The motion of me adjusting the chair closer to the table creates an atrocious grating, and the sound causes them all to laugh.

"Dear Hope, this is my ward, Edgar. Edgar, this is the beautiful Hope I have spoken so fondly of," he says to the young boy beside him.

Although it's odd he does not introduce both children, I acknowledge the introduction and smile across the table. "Hello, Edgar. I am pleased to make your acquaintance."

Before I finish my sentence, I'm met with warm smiles from all. From their similarities in terms of age and appearance, I assume they're fraternal twins. Each has dark brown hair and eyes, with eyebrows to match. The young girl dons a forest-green dress with a matching age-appropriate bonnet, while Edgar wears a suit tailored from the same fabric. Even though they both must be well under the age of ten, the richness of their outfits makes them resemble miniature adults.

Interrupting my moment of assessment, David opens his mouth to interject. "Edgar's arrival was almost comical. I didn't expect him until later in the week, but a carriage—I dare say one similar in appearance to yours—arrived, and the driver shoved him out the door," he states with a laugh.

Hiding my worry, I open my eyes wide with gleeful surprise and forcefully curl my lips into a smile. "How curiously amusing."

Glimpsing across the table, I notice Edgar staring at me, his expression off-putting. The little chap resembles a smaller version of Daniel. His tiny grin is identical to his father's and sends chills trickling down my spine.

Noticing my stare, he angrily looks at David and opens his perfectly sculpted lips to speak. "David, did you forget something or should I say, someone?"

"Oh, yes, of course. I apologize for my oversight. Hope, please meet Edgar's twin sister, Louise," David says with a smirk and a chuckle.

"We've heard so much about you, miss," Edgar states, confidently leaning forward after refocusing his glare in my direction. The facetious nature of David's introduction was a bit perplexing, and the young boy's demand and reply radiate condescension and entitlement. Edgar's intonation is so unsettling that it prompts the smile to fade from my lips.

"Is that so?" I reply, pretending to care.

The young boy frantically nods, then unapologetically kicks his sister under the table. An anxious look consumes her face as she winces from the pain; then she joins in, nodding in agreement.

"Yes," Louise says, staring at the table.

Taking a cue from the girl, I try to find something to distract myself and reach for the chalice in front of me to quench my parched throat. Afterward, I don't recall a single drop touching my lips, yet the cup is empty.

How odd, I think, trying to determine whether my empty cup was an oversight or if I finished the drink without remembering.

David notices my confusion. "Let me call the waitstaff to fill our cups," he says, then signals for the butler.

After they exchange a few inaudible whispers, the butler leaves and soon returns with an open bottle of red wine, which he pours into David's cup. The crimson liquid jolts my mind back to the memory of knocking over the bottle in my reoccurring dream. Night after night, the dream has haunted me: I'm at Daniel's estate, twirling in my ornate wedding dress, and like clockwork, the full skirt tips the wine bottle, spilling the red liquid all over the hardwood floor. It's always disturbing how the red pool mimics seeping blood; the very thought makes me grimace.

The sound of the butler filling my cup snaps me out of my reminiscence, and I snatch the drink from the table. Noticing me holding my glass in the air, David raises his to match mine and smiles. After we finish our silent toast, I quickly drink the substance to calm my nerves. I wipe the residue from my lips, and within moments the room spins around me. Placing my hands on the table, I try to focus.

What is wrong with me? I frantically wonder.

The sound of glassware and plates shattering around me causes my shoulders to flinch so forcefully that my chair nearly topples. The loud crashing noises continue to ring throughout the great dining hall for what seems an eternity. I try to speak, but nothing comes out.

"Dav..." I say, panic filling my eyes.

The ability to articulate my words has left, along with the oxygen from my lungs. Through my fading coherence, I make out the image of David's unconscious body hunched over the table in front of him. Glass shards surround the eloquently disheveled place setting and blood spills to the floor. The euphoric feeling of floating feels familiar to me, and the recollection makes me grab for the locket around my neck. Frantically I fumble to open the metal, and my discovery sends me into a state of distress: nothing scatters to the porcelain plates. The poppy seeds have vanished, and the epiphany sends me into a frenzy.

Oh, God, is this the end? I think of the others I sedated with the seeds and what they must have felt in their last minutes on earth.

Concerned about the adolescents' response to the traumatic events, I struggle to focus on them across the way. No matter how hard I try, only one child comes into sight, and it is Edgar. Rather than his eyes viewing the traumatic event unfolding before him, Edgar sits smiling with gaze fixated on the room's corner. Feeding off his glee, a demonic laugh sounds from the shadows, and my twitching eyes turn to glance in the direction of the small boy's happiness. Thrust into a state of silent hysterics, unable to move or make a sound, I sit helplessly catatonic, as though I'm a tranquilized animal.

Is it possible he can see like me? The thought runs through my mind.

With my eyes fixed across the table, the heartbreak from David's demise sets in, and tears stream from my eyes as each vein in my heart rips from my chest wall. Without warning, I fall into a state of hopelessness. My brain gives up fighting to stay awake, and I allow the wind to be taken from my lungs. As I witness the beauty of David's soul exiting his body, I visualize myself floating beside him. He glides through the shadows and laughs as he joins the children. Before my skull crashes against the table, they wave at me with slight grins burned into their lips.

"Sleep tight, child," the shadow states with profound sincerity.

Feeling my soul adrift, I wonder who will look after the tiny creature being left behind in this world. As my vision continues its final descent into the afterlife, I hear light footsteps coming toward me. Etched with blurry lines, Edgar lowers his face beside my resting head and watches his reflection in my glassy pupils. He then smugly draws forth a smile on his seemingly youthful face.

"*Mors tua, vita mia,*" he says with a sadistic cackle.

Contradicting his tone, he reaches forward, and I feel a slight pressure on my eyelids as he kindly closes them for me. The meaning of his words prompts a final smile to form across my dying lips, and dwelling in a world of darkness feels therapeutic to me. Thank God I'm free and can finally sleep in peace.

EPILOGUE

To those conflicted or curious:

Since I know how much you value my opinion, I am certain you are dying to hear my assessment regarding how the grand finale transpired. I will express that you should never have shed a tear for my fading presence within the bleak yet pleasant narrative we joyously shared, for I can say with certainty; that I did not. Like everything in life, all things must tragically end, and if I steadfastly did not pity the journey I selected for myself, neither should you. Regardless of the outcome, I am not sad nor mad; I am glad.

When I considered doing the work of the shadow, I weighed out every option afforded me and my aspirations before making a decision. It was blatantly clear that each winding facet of the storyline would follow the strict guidelines put forth by the entity's ever-changing whims. Upon completing my decision to embark upon the Shadow's quest, I took a moment of solace to banish my naivety like a reptile shedding its skin. You may wonder what that encompassed. Well, it entailed profoundly reflecting on the pitfalls of trading in my storyline for a chance for differentiating societal treatment.

Now that I am deceased and no longer bound to my commitment, I can freely speak on several topics I believe still make my soul restless. I had no prior knowledge of the specifics of my family's demise, but I knew a bit more than I initially shared with you and thought it necessary to confess if I wish to sleep in peaceful slumber. Contrary to my initial claim of being naive to my family's impending fate, I was aware of the potential for darker times and each of their deaths. I will ask you one pertinent question before you determine my quick disregard for their lives as a monstrosity. What would your threshold be for severe mistreatment? Don't coat your sinister thoughts with sugar to make yourselves less guilty over your dark contemplation.

If you were to ask me the same question, I would answer without hesitation that those wretched people, referred to as my birth family, crossed my threshold for abuse beginning the day of my birth. During my almost eighteen-year existence in their care, perhaps what sealed their treachery most was the continuous throwing of sinful words at me like stones. It was not my fault, and I blame every one of their small jabs for pushing me to the point of retaliation. Their actions forcefully pried my naive eyes open, so I was able to see the Shadow and address their corrupt ways. Regardless of the outcome, no matter how grim, I would not have done anything differently.

Another topic I shall like to spill light on revolves around my abrupt departure. You may have wondered how such a surprise ending to my life translated into something so peaceful in my mind. When most face their last moments of life before death, panic can ensue with thoughts of unsettled desires. At first, I did ponder the life I may have led with the attractive man sitting across the table from me. Then suddenly, the reality of our short timeline together set in, and I questioned if my intrigue was only a situation of convenience. We did not share each other's company long enough to inquire about his family history or discover his true character. The man could have been a bloody con for all I knew; nonetheless, I will cherish the spark we shared in all fairness.

It was not our relationship or its potential that brought me comfort. If anything, I noticed myself searching for solace in anything other than myself. As my vision began drifting away at the dinner table, I found a strange familiarity in the pupils of that disturbed child's glare. Yes, Edgar's eyes brought my soul a complex sense of fulfillment. His gaze seemed to encompass the presence of the shadow, but not in the capacity you may expect. I am confident the pretentiously polished child was crafted of the mysterious being's flesh, meshed into one. Unlike my experience of being guided by a separate entity, he had been inhabited. At that moment, I was quite aware I had run out of options, checkmate, it had won. The advising source had claimed victory over my mortality for the last time, and I was more than happy to relinquish every last breath to free my soul from the hellish purgatory.

Everything in life comes at a cost, whether big or small. Towards the end, I found the tole being charged by my shadowy friend more significant than my given life. In my final breaths, I wanted nothing more than to escape its engulfing control and it was explicitly clear that freedom from the darkness was impossible as long as my heart kept time. My heart's finished beat seemed my only option for regaining the independence I longed to possess.

There is one thought still lingering in my mind. I occasionally wonder what happened to those poor children left without a parental figure and how they became wrapped up with the same beckoning call as I. Upon my first assumptions, I believed them to be young and unable to comprehend the repercussions of selling one's soul for fulfillment of desires. Being twins, I questioned whether both children signed onto the murderous lifestyle or just Edgar alone. The dynamic grasps my attention and piques my experimental interest.

Let me ask you a question. What would you choose if a mysterious man or woman offered you the world for an indeterminate fee? Might you willingly take the offer or stay stagnant in the misery of your impoverished ways? Now, if you are speaking, stop. Don't bother stating your answer aloud. Think to yourself alone in the confines of a quiet room. Before you depict your core as better than ours, blow out all candles lighting your room and sit in pitch-black darkness, close your eyes, and listen closely for the shadow to speak. Upon hearing its voice, I assure you that your answer will metamorphose into something more authentic to your bones. That is the only way to weed out the societal influence from your thoughts and listen to notions I think to be less bland. We are confident what path you would haphazardly select if it alleviated your challenges, even if only temporarily.

Reflecting on the only living bodies left in the room, I hope, for their sake, they understand the implications associated with giving your only vessel to such a monstrosity. Without the barrier between the two souls, there is nowhere to hide from fear or vile nature. Sheer avoidance is the safest route for those who treacherously cross their path. If you pray, you should start now, and if not, you had better run. If you find yourself in complete desperation, whisper my name, Hope Bonnet, I shall try to respond. Concerning Edgar and Louise, I welcome you with open arms if not too lost in the pits of eternal flames. May God help save your soul.

Heed my warning,

ABOUT AUTHOR

Gitte Tamar

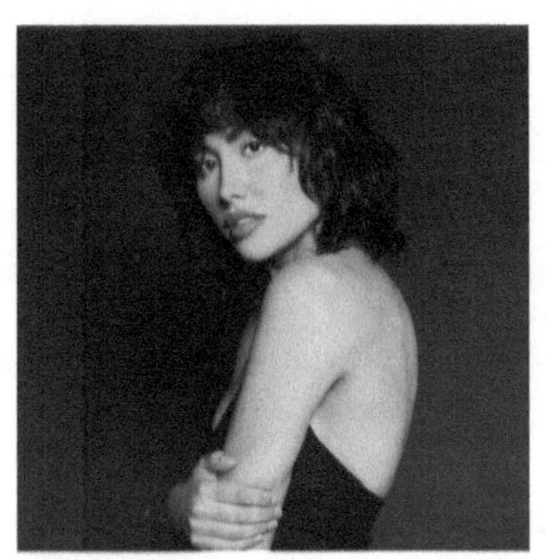 Brigitte, "Gitte," Tamar was born in a small rural Oregon town. Growing up, she was enthralled by scary tales featuring poetic tones and consistently gravitated towards writing darkened narratives. In *Shadows That Tempt*, Brigitte continues to explore *the stigma of mental illness in the format of a psychological thriller.* Shadows That Tempt *is the second installment of* The Shadows That Speak trilogy.